David VanCura

The Chronicles Of L.J. Stevans, Book 1

David VanCura

The Chronicles Of L.J. Stevans, Book 1

Truth and Transformations

JustFiction Edition

Impressum/Imprint (nur für Deutschland/only for Germany)
Bibliografische Information der Deutschen Nationalbibliothek: Die Deutsche Nationalbibliothek verzeichnet diese Publikation in der Deutschen Nationalbibliografie; detaillierte bibliografische Daten sind im Internet über http://dnb.d-nb.de abrufbar.
Alle in diesem Buch genannten Marken und Produktnamen unterliegen warenzeichen-, marken- oder patentrechtlichem Schutz bzw. sind Warenzeichen oder eingetragene Warenzeichen der jeweiligen Inhaber. Die Wiedergabe von Marken, Produktnamen, Gebrauchsnamen, Handelsnamen, Warenbezeichnungen u.s.w. in diesem Werk berechtigt auch ohne besondere Kennzeichnung nicht zu der Annahme, dass solche Namen im Sinne der Warenzeichen- und Markenschutzgesetzgebung als frei zu betrachten wären und daher von jedermann benutzt werden dürften.

Coverbild: www.ingimage.com

Verlag: JustFiction! Edition ist ein Imprint der
LAP LAMBERT Academic Publishing GmbH & Co. KG
Heinrich-Böcking-Str. 6-8, 66121 Saarbrücken, Deutschland
Telefon +49 681 37 20 310, Telefax +49 681 37 20 310-9
Email: info@justfiction-edition.com

Herstellung in Deutschland:
Schaltungsdienst Lange o.H.G., Berlin
Books on Demand GmbH, Norderstedt
Reha GmbH, Saarbrücken
Amazon Distribution GmbH, Leipzig
ISBN: 978-3-8454-4544-1

Imprint (only for USA, GB)
Bibliographic information published by the Deutsche Nationalbibliothek: The Deutsche Nationalbibliothek lists this publication in the Deutsche Nationalbibliografie; detailed bibliographic data are available in the Internet at http://dnb.d-nb.de.
Any brand names and product names mentioned in this book are subject to trademark, brand or patent protection and are trademarks or registered trademarks of their respective holders. The use of brand names, product names, common names, trade names, product descriptions etc. even without a particular marking in this works is in no way to be construed to mean that such names may be regarded as unrestricted in respect of trademark and brand protection legislation and could thus be used by anyone.

Cover image: www.ingimage.com

Publisher: JustFiction! Edition
is an imprint of the publishing house
LAP LAMBERT Academic Publishing GmbH & Co. KG
Heinrich-Böcking-Str. 6-8, 66121 Saarbrücken, Germany
Phone +49 681 37 20 310, Fax +49 681 37 20 310-9
Email: info@justfiction-edition.com

Printed in the U.S.A.
Printed in the U.K. by (see last page)
ISBN: 978-3-8454-4544-1

Table of Contents

The Chronicles of L.J. Stevans

For my wife Melanie and daughter Alisha. You are my driving force in life.
Thank you for the love and inspiration you have given me.

To my parents, Kim and Joe. You have shown me how to be a husband and father.
It is through both your successes as well as your failures that I have been shown the way.

To all my brothers and sisters I proudly served next to in the Army.
I have learned many of life's lessons from you all, how listen and be a leader.
Never forget the people and ideas we fight for.

The Chronicles of L.J. Stevans: Part 1. Introducing L. J.

Hello World,

My name is L.J. Stevans. I am what you might refer to as a world traveler, or maybe to some, a drifter. I have done and seen a great many things during my travels. But before I get deeper into that and about who I am, I have a few questions I would like to ask you. What is "greatness"? How does one achieve "greatness"? Who determines if the things you do, or your life in general is/was "great"? I and some of the things I have done during my time have been referred to as "Great", but what does it mean? I'm not a man that enjoys *overly* boasting about his past, present or future deeds to others. However, I am a man that enjoys telling a story, the fact that I am centered around most of the stories is of course merely coincidence. At least in my mind it is. In truth I am just a man that for some reason, habitually finds himself in the right place at the right time, or depending on your position in the event, the absolute wrong place at the very worst time. I seem to have a tendency to find adventure no matter the situation. Aside from sharing my life with a world I have often had to live on the fringes of. I do have a secondary motive for beginning these chronicles. I know that records from the past are not easy to come by. So call this me doing my part to ensure that future generations have a sense of how we lived during our time.

I have traveled all over the world and have seen amazing wonders, things you wouldn't believe...... things I'm not sure even *I* believe myself. What I can say is everything I or others may tell you about my life and the events therein is a 100 percent true account as they or I see it. But, that's the kicker, isn't it? Most events that take place in the world are seen from many different vantage points. Some accurate, some askew, but all of them, at least in the minds of the people doing the recounting are true. The way they saw it, is for all intensive purposes the way it happened. It's funny when you think about it. One hundred people can witness the same event but when asked about it, you are likely to get one hundred different accounts. In my case I just tell it how I lived it, and through it all I have been labeled with many descriptions of who I am, a hero, a villain, a thief, an acquirer of goods and services (if there is a difference between the last two), an adventurer, a businessman and many other titles I am sure you will hear when others describe who I am. The one thing everyone who has ever met me will agree upon is that I, regardless of the title labeled onto me, am painfully honest to a fault. In the end it truly does not matter what others think of a man just as long as he knows who he is. I know exactly who I am. So allow me to fully introduce myself. I am L.J. Stevans and I am incapable of lying.

I think a great number of people would view my condition as a good thing. At least when they are on their side of conversations with me, simply because there is no wondering about things. You ask, I tell, simple as that. However, if you take a moment to think about what it would be like if you could never again utter an untrue word, nor tell the smallest of fibs. Never able to spare someones feelings with the use of a little white lie. I think many of you would view it as the burden it truly can be. To me it is just the way I am. And since I do not know any other way of life, I really don't have an opinion about it either way, save the way the truth makes me feel when someone hears it, especially the hard to except truths. Let me make one other thing clear, I am talking about truth here, not being correct all the time, I am just as capable of being wrong as you are. I am just always truthful. Trust me there is a huge difference between the two. It's funny to think just how many people have sought me out thinking I "knew" something or was psychic, if there is such a thing. No friends I do not "know" any more than the next guy. Now the effects of my condition and the things I have gained or more importantly lost from being born this way however, I do have opinions on and that in part is why I am here today talking to all of you. What I know for certain is that this *gift* has saved my life on more than one occasions. However, due to the fact that it has also put my life in jeopardy many times over, it can often feel like a curse. It will be interesting to say the least to dive back into my exploits of the past. In some cases it will also be very painful. In reality it is like anything else, it has its positives and negatives. It's just that when we are talking about truth it is often the extreme of either of the two.

You see many years ago when I was born, I was so, without the ability to lie. Now of course that didn't become evident to me or my family until years later, when the way I spouted the truth could not simply be written off as an innocent child's insights. Still, it took me to lose my family to the truth to understand the gravity of my condition.... Ah Yes, I remember the day as well as would you, if you suddenly discovered that your Father was a killer. Now he may have taken my Mother from me, but it *appeared* that it was my inability to tell anything but the truth that took the rest of my family from me. Which I hindsight would turn out to be a very fortunate thing for me, being that it saved me from their true nature. However it also left me on my own in the world at a young age to carve out my own path, it left me...alone. Where it is not only where I found I belong, but would also lead me to discover my true purpose in life.

Even though I have many siblings, they were older and were starting their next phases in life. So the house I grew up in would mainly consist of myself and my parents. My Mother and Father seemed to love one another passionately, until I started to hear rumblings that one of them also found passion outside their marriage as well. I was 14 when I was asked if I knew my Mother was sleeping around, without even a second thought I uttered the yes that would alter my life and ultimately end my Mothers. When my Uncle Thomas asked me the question I knew the answer would get back to my Father, after all they were twins. I find it odd now, he didn't even let me explain that all I had to go on was rumors, so "knowing" was a stretch. It's like he knew the answer to the question and just......needed my yes......Strange. One of the many things that were beyond my anticipation of abilities was what would come next. I never expected what I would find upon coming home from school, in fact to this day it still seems like a distant nightmare unwilling to fully vacate my memories. I walked through the front door and there it was...... my Father was strangling the last bit of life from her. This would be the first time I felt fear so strong I could not react to the events unfolding before me. To this day I believe that if I could have dealt with that fear, or even returned home even sooner than I did that I may have been able to save her. Instead I just stood there frozen in disbelief and terror. Because of this I vowed never again would I be so affected by fear in the face of danger, I would right the wrongs I witnessed from then on, no matter the cost.

My Father noticed I was there, and as if on cue he burst into tears and begged me not to say anything to anybody. "I don't know what happened", he cried to me. "I was just confronting her about what you told Thomas and the next thing I knew I was overcome with rage", he rationed through his tears. Odd that he said that, as if he was trying to pass a part of the blame on to me. "Do not tell anyone outside of the family about what really happened to her, I'll take care of it L.J., I'll make this right." Thinking back on it now, what a funny thing he said to me, on a few levels if you think about it. I mean how could this be made right? And just why was I expected to blindly protect my Mothers murderer, Father or not? And why would he ask me a child, to protect him with a lie it turns out I could not even tell. He knew that I could not do what he was asking me, yet he still asked instead of just "getting rid" of me. Regardless of what he said to me after the fact, he knew what was going to happen when he confronted her, how could he not. The thing I find most humorous about that day is that he thought he could make it look like a suicide and he was so convinced the lie would work he called the police to the house himself, even before her body turned cold. Thinking back on it now and having the proper perspective that only time provides, it was an almost perfect little performance he put on for me...a*lmost* perfect. See I don't think *anyone* could have been more obvious and intentional with his actions and stories about what happened. No, he planned on being caught, it was just my actions that he was unable to predict correctly.

Once I saw the difference in his false grief to the officers that arrived at our home, I was convinced that something was off with my Father. It's that difference that made it even easier for me to contradict his claims. As it turned out in a funny twist of fate, the Policeman, Officer Jack Hundley, had a history with my Mother that no one knew about, one that went much deeper than the rumored affair she was having. So it didn't take much for him to figure out the truth for himself. But still of course he asked me what I saw and with a happy beat in my heart I confirmed his suspensions. This would be the first but certainly not the last time I would find myself straddling the line of perception. On one side I was being viewed a Hero for turning my Father over to the hands of the law. On the other, I was seen as a Judas for not keeping an ill-conceived loyalty to my Father, either way it cost me my family and it would not be the last time the truth would carry a steep price. As with any type of price, it would sometimes be easier to pay than others.

When I saw the hurt and betrayal in my Fathers eyes I knew it would not be the last I would see of him. The hurt seamlessly turned into confusion as to why his only son would so effortlessly turn his Father over to the law. He always knew I was incapable of lying yet he still showed confusion when I couldn't in his defense. Ether way, in his head it was still I that was the criminal for turning him in. Like he had already forgotten that it was his actions that led to my Mothers lifeless body laying on the floor before us. I will forever remember the last look he shot at me, it was the same icy gaze the rest of family shot my way once they found out what had happened and what I did, or in their mind what I didn't do, what I *supposed* to do.

You see for reasons I could not yet grasp, they were all blindly loyal to my Father and for that I was cast out on my own, 14, alone and abandoned. The things I would later discover about my family and their private deeds would provide me with the knowledge that not only was this not my Fathers first go at murder. But that also my Mothers death was not the whim it seemed to be, it was strategically planned and they all had a part to play in it, apparently I did too.......

......But that, that my friends is another story for another day. What I can say is that these events are what led to my decision to become a constant thorn in their side every opportunity that presented itself. But now, I need time to clear my thoughts, and I'm sure after reading my ramblings, your eyes may need to do the same. I ask for your forgiveness in advance if jumping around to different memories become the norm. You see this is the first time I have had to relive the events that shaped me into the man I am now and dwelling on one for too long just causes me grief I do not wish to experience again. I will make this promise right now however, all will be reveled in time. There is a lot to tell and many emotions that will once again be uncorked from the recesses of my mind. My journey is certainly not complete and with me going public with my past. I have little doubt that things may start to get interesting for me yet again.

What I can leave you with is this. The memory I just shared with you is the one that would ultimately shape the rest of my existence. It would also serve as the lesson that the absolute truth always has a price and that price is usually loneliness in one form or another. Thank you for joining me here, I only hope I can provide you a bit of perspective, and hopefully a hint of entertainment. Just remember (even though this is counter to the things we are preached to as children) lying only hurts if you get caught, but the truth in some cases can alter your world forever.

L.J. Stevans

The Chronicles of L.J. Stevans: Part 2. A Public Thank You to a Hero

Dear Mr. L.J. Stevans,

My name is Alexandra Fueller, I have been quietly looking for you for years to express my thanks to you. So when I found this ….. running forum of yours, I knew I had to share our encounter with the world. I think that is long over due for you to share your adventures with the public. I can only hope that the rumored darker side of your past doesn't catch up to you because of it. For a very long time I would hear the occasional tale of things you have done since you left our town, some good and some not so flattering. But I guess it just depends on whom is telling the stories that determine in what way you are viewed. There have been a few passing men in our town who seem to be on the more shady side of the law, that talk about how you ruined their plans and such. it never fails to bring a smile to my face and remind me of what you did for us and me in particular. As for the stories that paint you in a different light....well.. I am sure that when you are ready all will be explained . Whatever is said, it still will never change the way I or my family view the man you are.

It's been more than 30 years since I last saw you but your impact on my, my family's and my towns lives is still felt today. I will never forget the day you walked into our town of Milton, it was my 16th birthday and if not for you it would have most certainly been my last.

You see my Father worked very hard to keep all 7 of us clothed and fed and sheltered. He worked the Coal Mines on the out skirts of our town for more than 15 years only to get cast aside when a new management bought out the Mines. It was at that point he turned to gambling and petty crimes. He worked for a local thief by the name of William, who had his hands in just about any criminal activity that took place in the area. The gambling never seemed to work in my Fathers favor and that led to him doing "jobs" for William. There was a line my Father would not cross however. When he refused to do as William said, he was told there would be a price for his refusal and his youngest child (me) would be the one to pay it. My Father tried to get us out of town which seemed to only enrage William more. Because of it my Father wanted to not celebrate my 16th Birthday in the town square with our neighbors. Which is a long running tradition. My Mother on the other hand, insisted that we had to get back to a state of normalcy. However, my Father knew that William would make his move during the party, he said William was like a showman in that way. He wanted everyone to see what the penalty was for going against his will. It turns out my Mother should have heeded my Fathers words.

The party went off without delay and it seemed like everything was going just fine, and that is when you arrived Mr. Stevans. It is hard to forget a man that interrupts your Birthday and steals one of your gifts off the table and flees the scene. We were about to give chase when my   Father halted us, he must have sensed what you clearly knew. As I started to protest and insistent that we follow you, and turn you in to the police, we heard an explosion. We were quick to investigate and ran 2 streets down to find you sprawled out in the road with the package in charred pieces a mere 15 feet from you. We knew then what you did, what we didn't know was why a man would risk his life like that for strangers.

When you awoke in the hospital 3 days later, I was there. I wanted to be the first person you saw. Call it a 16 year old's first crush, how could any young girl not fall for a handsome man that just saved her life. Of course I knew you were too old for me but at that age a crush is a crush and a girl could always dream. When you gathered yourself you asked if anyone else was hurt. To that I replied "Thanks to your actions, no." When I asked you why you saved me and how you knew about the firebomb. You cryptically told me you were simply in the right place at the right time, and you made it your business to learn things upon arriving in a new town.

A week later you arrived at our door to inform us you were well enough to move on and that William and his men would no longer be a problem. You then handed a large envelope to my Father, and a single red rose with a bow around it for me. You then kissed my hand and wished me a belated Happy Birthday, with that you were gone.

To this day I don't know what you said to my father or what was in the envelope or how you handled William. What I do know, however, is that never again would we see or hear from William, nor would we want for food or money. I may never know why you did the things you did but you Sir are a hero to me and my family. To this day I still have that rose pressed between the pages of my favorite book. It took till yesterday when I read your post for me to learn about your inability to lie. I've heard stories of course, but I thought it was just that, a story. I once heard of a man who could ONLY lie, but that I know must be false, who could live that way. Maybe you have heard of him in your travels.

In closing, Mr. Stevans I just want to offer you a heartfelt thank you, and I am thrilled to be the first in what I am sure will be a long line of people wanting to share your deeds with the world.

Stay Safe,

Alexandra Fueller

The Chronicles of L.J. Stevans: Part 3. Responding to Alexandra Fueller

Hello Again World,

I was not originally going to post another tale until tomorrow but after reading the words Alexandra wrote earlier...... I had to respond. It brought me back to a series of firsts for me. It was the first time I had ever been to Milton, the first time I ever crashed a party. It was also the first craziest thing I had ever done. Along with the first, but certainly not the last time I would put myself in danger even when my instincts were to run the other way.

I was still a young man at the time, no more than 23 years old, truth be told this was actuality the first real adventure that I was on my own for. Before this time, Jack didn't want me out on my own. He said there were too many people looking for me, so he was always at my side.....Well I guess technically I was at his side, but why split hairs.

Even before I learned about Alexandra and her family, I knew of William and the troubles that faced the town of Milton. You see after I discovered the true nature of my family (which I promise you all I will get into when the time is right, for the moment lets just refer to them as criminals in nature). I started to look into their contacts and determining if I needed to intervene or not. In most cases I would indeed throw myself into the frying pan. Even against the urging of the practical side of my brain. I do not make the claim to be a brave man or a great fighter or adventurer. I just can't seem to turn away the opportunity to right a wrong. Even more so when it, even in the least involves my Family.

It wasn't hard to find William upon my arrival, in fact I found him in the first bar I entered. I would later discover that when a criminal does not hide away, but instead leaves himself in the wide open, it is usually for 1 of 2 reasons. He is either stupid, or as it was the case with William, confident and well connected. By this time my name was becoming known for both good and bad reasons, depending on how you look at it. I found that my status as a wild card would be a good thing in the minds of most shady characters. When you have the kind of power William and men of his ilk possess, you tend to not trust the people who appear all "bad", for the simple reason as the man who is all "bad" will more than likely turn against you when it suits him the most. Nor do you trust those with the reputation of being all "good". And really it's for the same reason as not trusting or keeping permanent company of men you view as smarter than yourself. Because they, at some point will see the best opportunities to take what they "think" is entitled to them. In either scenario you are out of a job at some point, and more than likely dead. So these men in power love to work with people such as myself. People who appear to be straddling the fence of good and bad, because they can serve your purposes the best. Quite simply because in most cases they are only truly interested in the same thing that drives most men of my perceived status.....monetary gains .

When I arrive in a place and I need information fast, I use that blurred reputation I built to acquire it. Within 45 minutes I had spoken to and gambled with almost all of Williams men and within an hour I was able to earn an audience with the man himself. I was viewed by him as a passer by looking for a way to fill my pockets before I moved on, and once we got around to the heart of my visit and I revealed my true Family name.....well....then I was afforded all the information I required.

I saw the present with the fire bomb within it , and knew it's purpose after my conversation with William. Funny at one point I almost had him convinced to allow me to deliver it, but I thought better of that course of action and figured it was better to let the box with a bomb in it to leave the room before I made my move on William. Since this was the first time I was actually putting my life in danger, I felt it was best to use the easiest and most basic tactic available, intimidation. For the first time I leaned on my Families reputation to scare a group out of town, I even got him to pay me off before he left, most, but certainly not all of which I would later give to Alexandra's family. In reality I knew it was a dangerous ploy to use my Families name to scare off someone, and due to the fact I would learn soon after this event that doing so would catch up with me and have near fatal consequences, I wouldn't be using such tactics again.

After feeling secure in the fact that William would indeed be moving his operations out of Milton, I knew I had little time to waste if I wanted to intercept his "little birthday surprise". So off to the Town Square and Alexandra's party I ran. I saw the celebration was reaching its peek and soon the gifts would be opened. It was then I knew I would have to put myself in real danger and snatch the gift and run from public reach with just hope that this token of Williams "affection" wouldn't erupt in my face. After I made the grab and dash, I got out of sight quickly and threw the package away from me in a safe direction just as it was about to explode. I managed to only get a tad singed and a concussion from the ordeal. However I knew there was a good chance that someone from the party would give chase after the "thief" disrupting a birthday in the manner I did. So before I blacked out I could only hoped they would see my true intentions and give aid instead of ......well you know, killing me as a thief right there in the road, which as most of you know can happen in the harsh reality we live in.

I awoke some time later in a hospital, with a beautiful young woman sitting at my bed side. Whom I quickly identified as the Birthday girl from the events that led to me being in this hospital bed. Although I knew she was far too young for me, beauty is still beauty. She had amazing eyes, very deep and blue. Her hair was flawlessly taken care of with long flowing blonde locks accenting her face. Truly it would have been a shame to let a beauty like hers be burned away by a fire bomb. After a little friendly banter about the safety of the other guests, she asked the age old question of WHY. I explained to her I had a tendency to be in the right place at the right time, and that I had a way of learning about my surroundings when in a new location, and she seemed satisfied with my answer.

When I was well enough to travel I went to Alexandra's house to deliver a single rose to her as a replacement present for the one I "stole". As well as an profitable envelope to her Father, along with a reminder that I would keep my ear open to hear if he has fallen back into crime. If so, no matter what the circumstances, our next meeting would not be as pleasant. With that I was off, back on the road to a new destination. It didn't take long for my exploits in Milton to come around full circle with the intention of biting me in the most uncomfortable of places......but that friends again is a story for another time. For now just know that this would not be the last I saw of William, and he would see to it that my life would indeed take another turn into a very dark place. There is always a price for your actions, and indeed the price I would later pay would be more than I could bare.

I wanted to close this entry with first a message to you Alexandra. It means a great deal to me that you kept the memento I gave you all these years, and I was happy to be of assistance. Also to answer your question about the man with the opposite affliction of my own. Yes I have heard the stories of his existence, and I pray they are what they are, just stories. Because if a man like that truly exists he would easily be the most sinister and dangerous man in the world. If you ask me though, his existence does not seem probable, I mean I don't think a man like that could function in today's world. Then again I wonder how many people have said the same about me over the years upon hearing my tales. Perhaps one day the answer will reveal itself.

Again thank you all for joining me here in these chronicles and I just can't wait to see what tomorrow will bring. In fact the day I stop yearning for another day of possible adventure or reminiscence of adventures past, is the day I no longer wish to inhabit this world. Till next time friends.

L.J. Stevans

The Chronicles of L.J. Stevans: Part 4. Getting to Know L.J.

Hello Again World,

So far I must say recalling the past has been.....interesting to say the least. The fears I may have had, just a few years ago about going public with my story, have diminished greatly. As I advance in years, I have a greater appreciation for my life. Stories that people may hear and pass on about me are one thing. However, I feel as this is the right time to share my past with the world, set the record straight and work to preserve our past for future generations. I can only hope that my past exploits will teach and entertain...... for those of you interested anyways.

Being able to reconnect with people from my past can be a wonderful but dangerous thing. Not everyone I have encountered in my travels hold me in as high regards as Alexandra does. I have been at lots of places, helped as many as I have been able to as well as helping myself along the way of course. I have never had just one true focus in my life, there have been many, love, revenge, money, and the search for the truth.

After my Mother was murdered before my eyes, I knew I had to make the difference in the world that I was incapable of in that moment. Fear froze me for the first time that day, when I needed to act most I could not and it haunts me to this very day. I knew from that day on that my life would be a lonely road, but one I was more than willing to walk. The biggest problem with helping people in perilous situations is that in most cases, though you may have helped the person you were intending, you also have just made another enemy with the people you stopped. The one thing I certainly did not need was more enemies but if I were to be ready for the trials ahead I needed to right the wrongs that were within my reach. But that comes later, to understand the things to come we must return to where it all began.

Even by the age of 14, I was someone who had a tendency to discover things. Most people talked to me openly, even though I was just a boy. Not being able to say anything but the truth was nothing but problems for me during adolescence. Even more so when others started to figure out my affliction. Once it became apparent, it didn't take long for my family to exploit it. They would all ask me questions about one another, which was my first inclination that something was.....off about them. A family with that level of mistrust even for one another is never a good, fully functioning one. As a boy it was more difficult to pick up on the things transpiring outside the house with them. I knew the older I got the more I would become aware to such things. Due to the fact that I was the only male child. Grooming me for my future and role in the Family would begin soon

That all changed when I began hearing rumors from school and from around town that my Mother got around behind my Fathers back. Things I wish would not have passed through my ears. Once I learned about my Mothers perceived infidelity I knew it was just a matter of time before I knew I would be asked about it, and once that happened I knew my life would shatter like a mirror. When my Uncle Thomas asked me about my Mother, for the first time I struggled against my nature, I wanted to lie, but there was nothing I could do. If a question is asked I must answer it with 100% truth, no exceptions. It's like a reflex, that's the best way to describe it, like a rubber mallet to the nerve in your knee. So like a mirror my life would indeed shatter. Though I tried to pick up the broken pieces of my proverbial mirror, every shard I grabbed would have a different reflection in it. Reflections of all the people I would later find to be involved in her Murder.

After I was cast out by my Family, I, in a way started to collect others. Officer Jack Hundley, the man who arrested my Father for the slaying of my Mother was not only my first real father like connection, but would also become my first teacher about the ways of the world. Aside from becoming a second Father to me he also had a love for my Mother and knew her in a way I never could. I knew her as the quiet yet loving person she was in our house. She appeared as almost a picture perfect counter part to my Father. It wasn't till after her death that I learned it was all smoke and mirrors. My Mother was not like the rest of my Family. All they wanted from life was power and control, two things they would do anything for to achieve. They didn't care who they hurt as long as they got what they wanted. All my mother wanted, however was out. That's where Jack came in. He and my Mother fell in love while working together to take the family down, they were growing too powerful and becoming far too big a problem for the region. Jack opened my eyes to this, and it was from the knowledge he gave me that I would base the rest of my life on.

To think, that it all would begin because I came home early from school. If I had not, my life would seemingly have turned out much different and I would not be the man pouring his life out to you today.

A crime of passion is what my Father claimed after his attempt to cover her death as a suicide failed. It turns out this was not how my mother was supposed to die. The family, I would soon discover had a plan for her, one that would exclude them from suspicion. The exact details, to this day are hazy at best. What I do know, however is that my Father, at the mercy of his emotions jumped the gun. All he needed was for me to corroborate his story and when I did not do so, a crime of passion became his defense.

This is where the power of my Family started to become apparent. Even with all the things my Mother and Jack had on my Father, and coupled with her murder, he still was only given 20 years of confinement at most, in an almost resort of a prison. As angry as Jack and I were over this, at least we had a time frame. We had 20 years, just 240 months. A mere

7,304 short days to prepare me for the war we both knew was coming.

In the meantime I was going to be a thorn in the side of my Family at every turn. To do so I knew I would have to learn everything Jack could teach. And teach me is just what he did. Over our time together he taught me to fight, investigate, reason, use logic everything a man should know. Little did I know that he would become a Father to me along with my best friend and most trusted strategist and adviser.

A war indeed would come, one that still rages on today. I still do not have all the answers I have been searching for. If the truth is to be completely clear, many more tales still must be and will be told. And even more must still be lived. I may have decided to take you back and enlighten you to my beginnings, but the end is still ways off. For now, however I hope some of the questions you no doubt have are answered. More answers still must be brought to the light of day. In the end the darkness will be lifted...... Till next time.

L.J. Stevans

The Chronicles of L.J. Stevans: Part 5. A Message Sent/ A Response

Mr. L.J. Stevans,

   You would be wise from this moment on to watch the things you decide to post. WE are watching, and not all of us are as friendly as I. We have met before and we will again down the road, the time is not yet set, but if your recent actions continue to ruffle the wrong feathers our rendezvous can and will occur much sooner. These truths you go about, do you really think it as cut and dry as you make it out to be? There is much you do not yet know, but you will learn I assure you. The end is inevitable, there is much to answer for. Do you think your words do not come with a cost? The truth ALWAYS has a price indeed, but are you willing to pay it Mr. Stevans?

--------------------------The next day----------------------------

Hello Again World,

   Good day everyone, I wanted to first address the general readers of these Chronicles. I wanted to assure to that in spite of the blatant threat I received yesterday, the truth will continue to be told. I do not respond well to threats and am certainly not easily scared off by them. I just wanted to let you all know that and also inform you that the statement below is not for the general readers but for the one responsible for yesterdays correspondence.

L.J. Stevans

To Whom it may concern,

   You may think that you can bully me out of speaking the truth, but you are quite mistaken. Even if I could keep the truth locked in, which of course you know I cannot, I wouldn't. These stories will continue to be shared and if you don't like it, well.... I welcome you to my home to attempt to silence me. Many have tried, so far none have succeeded. If you are truly arrogant enough to think I was not expecting a backlash to my decision to go public, and would not prepare accordingly, then you are not only arrogant but incompetent to boot. These are MY Chronicles, My life, My Journey, and I will not be robbed of control of them. Lastly and most pointedly, if you truly believe you are safe behind your anonymous stance, you are quite mistaken, your reach may indeed be far, but I am always prepared for the past to return. I guess now the true games will commence.

L.J. Stevans

The Chronicles of L.J. Stevans: Part 6. Light From The Darkness

Dear Friends,

I first want to begin today's post with this. I knew that probing through the past would be dramatic and emotional as well as eye opening for me. In fact it's the entire reason I decided to go public with it. Aside from strongly feeling the world should know what truly exists out there amongst them. However I never thought I would discover something as astounding as what I found today. You see, before I write in these Chronicles I look through my belongings, and what I have acquired over the years to help me decide what is most prominent and pertinent from my travels. I literally dig through the dark recesses that is my past to bring something back into the light for all to discover, as well as for me to relive. That all being said, I never thought I would stumble onto anything close to as life altering as to what I just uncovered. I must warn you, some of what you read ahead will be....hard to accept but I have very little doubt that every word of it is true.

After the family cast me out into the world alone, I slid back into the house to gather some of my belongings. In my searching I found a box with my mothers name on it in the basement. Naturally I took it and stored it away but never could bring myself to open it. Today I found the strength to do so, inside it amongst various items I found a book. It was my mothers favorite, her first edition of "The Wandering Man". A very obscure title written by an unknown author some 200 years ago. Pressed between the pages I found some papers, one of them a letter from my Mother addressed to me. This letter seems to have been written just hours before her untimely death. It is written in her hand and dated the same as the day of her murder. To be honest I have a few reservations about sharing this letter with the world, but I will do so. I told you all when I started this that I would not hold back anything relevant to my past and since this obviously qualifies as such I will disclose it to you all. Without further gilding the lily, lets begin.

My Dearest L.J.,

This is not the way I wanted to do this but I fear time is short. First I want you to know that I am aware about your condition, I always have been, I knew you would be born this way. All the men in my bloodline are, at least as far back as my Great Great Grandfather. Aside from you, since his time only three other men have been born in my family as odd as that my sound.

These men were my Great Grandfather, Grandfather and Father. So as unique as you are, through history you are not one of a kind, and if you sire any male children they will be born without the ability to lie as well. You will find that I have only written one letter and that is to you. The reason for that is that you are my only true child. You sisters are not my children, they are your Fathers from various past relationships. So any boys born from them will be able to lie and deceive you, it may be important for you to know that.

First, I know that your Uncle Thomas came to you asking about me and I also know that based on the rumors purposely spread to you, you could answer him in only one fashion. You need to know the entire ruse was set up with the purpose of trapping you into your Fathers and the Families grasp. They are planning to have me killed soon. I know that is the plan, they have discovered that I have been working with local and regional Authorities to bring down all the Families operations and I have accepted that death may be the consequence for my actions.

While I have not been as promiscuous as the rumors you heard have indicated. I have fallen in love with another, the Officer assigned to my case, and I can only hope that Jack will keep you safe after I am gone. The plan for my murder has changed over the last 24 hours and I know now it will be your Father who will do the deed, more than likely with the intention of you discovering him and I. He is going to use the event to guilt you into covering for him and making you feel that the Family is the only place you can go. If you do not back him I am not sure what the ramifications for you will be.

I do not know when or if you will discover this letter, but it should reach you shortly after my death as that was the instructions I gave to Jack, he is supposed to recover my possessions and store them. If it does not I can only hope Jack will be able to keep you safe, and give you the tools to live your life as you see fit. Jack will never rest until the Family is no more and he may ask you to aid him, if you do or not, that is your choice. How you live is completely up to you and that is the only gift I wanted to give you through all this....The choice.....A choice you would not have been granted if I stayed under your fathers rule. Vengeance is a lonely dangerous road. I would never wish that upon you Logan, live your life and do not waste it.

No matter who you have become or when you discover this letter, please know that my death was not your fault and that I love you unconditionally. And I know you are even more clever than I think you already to be. I believe you will see all the upcoming events for what they truly are. Lies and treachery will surround your life within the Family and I am sorry that you may have to live through that. Also I want you to know your Father was not the man he is now when we first met, or at least he did not appear as such. The truth is so hard to see now after all the lies and difficult truths that exist in our lives. I know you can come through all of this and do great things. Your Gift is the truth L.J. And when used properly it is a powerful weapon.

  Lastly I need you to know this most important bit of information about your Father and it will be hard to comprehend. You know strange things exist in the world, you and your condition are evidence to that. Still there are worse things out there, things much darker in nature and your Father is one such thing. He, along with his twin brother Thomas are....... immortal.....in a sense. Only one of them ages at a time, at this point it is hard to tell which of them is, but I know this to be the truth. I know that it happens in 20 year incriminates, and also there is something out there that allows them to reverse the aging process in some manner. I found journals of your Fathers in our Library hidden away, some dated back hundreds of years. I have also found sketches of him from over 300 years ago which I have provided you along with this letter as proof to my claims. Search hard my dear, you will find these claims to be true.

  I know this all has to seem like a great deal to you (even more so if you are still just a boy when you read this) as I have tried to shield you from the reality of the Families life. Your Father has done this with all his children. He feels that if you all are able to grow up in a state of normalcy and gradually be brought into the dealings of the Family, you will be more loyal to him. I just wanted you to grow up in a normal setting and tried to provide that. I feel as I have failed you but I can only hope this letter will shed the light you need to penetrate the darkness of these difficult times, as well as provide the clarity you will need to guide you in the future. You have the making of a great man Logan, never deny who you are. You may be able to hide from destiny for a short while but it will always catch up to you. I love you my son and always will live in your heart.

Your Loving Mother,

Lauren Janet Stevans.

  I truly am not sure of what to make of this letter. I mean Jack once asked me if I ever found a box or a book but never told me of what I would discover inside it. We will have to have a chat about this one. This letter is madness, I knew some things about what my Father had planned and who he truly was but …....this......this is just hard for me to grasp. I don't know if I could have handled this as a child. I'm not even sure I can handle it now. I have some hard choices ahead of me as fate and destiny have finally caught up with me just as Mother said it would. How does one accept the news that his family is full of supernatural beings? I have seen, wolf-men, beings that live only on blood and even bearded ladies but things that simply will not die, that's a new one for me. How does one take revenge of something that cannot die?

I suppose I will have to get creative. If there is one thing Jack and I have learned throughout the world is that *everything* has a weakness. Everything in nature does, it's simply a balance, so while I do not doubt that my Father is indeed Immortal, it's the definition that will have to be altered. I have lost too much in my life to allow him to go on forever, that much I know.

Father,

   I now know you are still out there and if so, you are reading this somewhere. Know this, you will see me again and you will answer for these things I have discovered in this letter. Up until now I have only been a pesky thorn in the Families side. Now it's time to bring it all down at your feet. For 40 years I have had questions in need of answering, perhaps now is the time to get them straight from your lips. That will come directly before I make you feel the ramifications of your treachery. If I have to make my way through the Family to accomplish this.....then so be it. I will figure out the answers to the question of Immortality, I will never stop, Father, until you pay for the life you have forced me to live.....In some ways it was a blessing but no child should have to be see the horrors of their Mothers murder.

For all you reading this,

   I know you may be confused by what you have just read. I know as do you that there are amazing things out there, things that defy logic but take it from me they are real. After everything I have seen in my travels I do not doubt believe what I have just learned. It would also help explain a few things about myself I have wondered about over the span of my life. By now you know that if I say something then I believe it must be true and I have seen enough in my time to bring credence to these latest discoveries. I must ask you to let go the accepted reality that you see around you. Squint hard and poke at the edges of the page and you will see the world for the incredible, visceral world it truly is.

   As uncertain as the future is, I still encourage any of you out there from my past to write in, not just to keep me grounded in this hectic time but also providing me the opportunity to call in some long standing favors. No doubt some of you have questions or maybe even answers to some of my own questions. Do not keep these things to yourselves, take this opportunity to break the silence of the abnormal life. It is time to illuminate the darkest corners of the world and our minds where the strangest and most dangerous truths lay. I do not know what will lay ahead, or what path I will now be forced to walk. However, I do know what is at the end of this path, and that soon it will be time to put my Fathers immortality to the test.

L.J. Stevans

The Chronicles of L.J. Stevans: Part 7. The Rule of A Stevans Sister/ A Plea for Help

To L.J. and all readers of these chronicles,

Hello everyone, my name is John Simmons and I live in the town of Gastings up by the Northern Lakes. I have been reading your tales Mr. Stevans. In doing so I realized that I, like so many out there knew your name and have heard of some of your past exploits. I also quickly identified with the name for a more ominous reason. I do not know if you are aware of the fact that one of your sisters, Bethany Stevans-Mason, along with her husband Desmond relocated here about 5 years ago and basically overran the region from the first day. Gastings like many towns up north is a fishing village and up until not surprisingly 5 years ago, we were a prosperous one. Then, seemingly overnight all of our vendors to the larger cities were bought out or replaced by a new transportation company known as A.M.D.S.. Almost instantly, distribution costs went up nearly 300 percent. Those of us that decided to venture out and move our product on our own were mercilessly attacked and our goods destroyed. The roads are no longer safe and fees and taxing are rumored to be bumped up yet again. The fisherman here tried to move farther north to avoid this group but their reach seems limitless. Anyone wanting to or that have attempted to leave have been "persuaded" to the thinking that it would be "in our families best interest to stay put". Even the most successful Captains are no longer profitable and Casino's and Burlesque houses are now the major businesses in town. Crime has grown rampant as more of us become desperate. We are all just months from complete personal and financial ruin.

I am writing you today in the hopes that with the information that has been revealed recently in these Chronicles. Combined with your own personal ties to the situation, you would be able to afford us some assistance. I know this is a long-shot but we are desperate up here Mr. Stevans and you are quite literally our last option if we are to save our Town. There are a number of us who are prepared to fight as a last resort. Some of us have roots here that go back multiple generations and I for one would rather die then see our town taken from us even more than it already has. We need leadership, someone of your reputation along with the connections you have. With that we can retake our lives. And with time and effort, be prosperous once again. We will wait no more than 2 weeks for help, after that period, we take our chances as well as our lives into our own hands and into battle. We have heard of stories in the past of your tendency to get involved in situations involving your Family and we only hope you are willing to do so one more time. We are clearly better off with you then without you and your actions will not be forgotten. In the uncertain times that so obviously lay before us and you in particular, friends and allies are not something you can afford to turn aside. I can only pray that we can make a difference and reclaim our futures. Your Family is beginning to turn into an unstoppable menace, with a reach and resources that seem limitless. Today, it's a fishing village but what will it be tomorrow? How many more will fall before this agent of destruction? I can't answer these questions, but you can provide clarity and perhaps the difference that we require.

With all our hope,

John Simmons

The Chronicles of L.J. Stevans: Part 8. The Liberation of Gastings

Forgive my haste everyone,

This is John Simmons, I wrote in asking L.J. for help with our Towns problems. My motives for this post is for multiple reasons. First and foremost, A heart felt thank you to L.J. Stevans and his allies. Gastings is free once again. His response to my plea was swift, he and his group of hero's rode into town on a mission and they achieved it....big time. My other reasons for this post are as follows. After meeting with L.J. and riding with him to Bethany's compound and confronting her we were separated. I don't know where he is or if he even made it out. I do know this however, both Bethany and her Husband now lay dead, it's the how that escapes me. Since L.J. has made it clear that this forum is like a note pad for history, I will share with you all the part of the story I witnessed with as much detail as I can recall.

It was took a mere six hours after I posted before the hero that is L.J. Stevans arrived in town with his band of friends. Upon meeting L.J. We shook hands and the first thing I noticed is the grip he has, strong, firm yet not intimidating, which really can also be used to describe not only his appearance but his demeanor as well. He was slightly above average height maybe 6"1, a slender yet well toned man to be sure and most certainly one of the most youthful looking men over the age of 50 I have ever met. Only small touches of gray accented his dark brown hair and short pointed beard and shaped mustache. He looked as he were plucked straight from a classic adventure film or off the cover of a book about heroic deeds and the such. He carried himself with a classic warriors grace, he moved agilely and with purpose. With him, at his side was a man quickly introduced to me and referred to as Jack which I can only assume was the very rarely seen Jack Hundley, L.J.'s mentor. He did not follow us going forward, he was there as a tactical adviser I believe and from the look of him, one would understand as to why. It's not that he appeared sickly ...... just well aged. After more quick introductions to and from our various accompany men, we formed a quick yet detailed plan, with that we and about 60 friends, were off.

From the moment we approached the A.M.D.S. compound L.J. was all business and filled with purpose. The glint in his gaze was telling and focused. He was a man focused and ready, I would not want to be opposite this man in battle. The compound was well guarded, but we still had the element of surprise as our ally even though I telegraphed our intent earlier via this blog. It would prove most beneficial, L.J. was adamant about not taking lives of the guards and the various security that dotted the grounds if at all possible. He explained that most of the men were more than likely recruited from our and a mixture of local towns from the region and were only employed by the Family due to a lack of options. Thus they would not hold much loyalty to their employers. As it turns out he was right, at least with the first 25 or so foes we encountered, they hardly put up a fight at all. We subdued them and later, after questioning they would be released. The next 15 or so men however would not be so accommodating. They fought hard but unorganized and due to our ambush style tactics were defeated with minimal damage to our group. It is kind of surprising that a group so powerful would employ such a lackluster defense. This is done either out of ignorance or confidence, either way we would capitalize on the advantage.

As we approached the central operating center of the compound, Bethany made her emergence. She stood before us in a flowing dark colored dress with a plunging neckline that emphasized her rather curvy if elder figure, her dark hair matched her cobalt black eyes. At the unexpected sight of her Brother she froze in place like a statue. A look of bewilderment and denial shot across her face. I wondered if this was the first time she had lain eyes on her brother in decades. I didn't have the chance to ask because as quickly as she appeared, fighting erupted in a side hallway and she used that distraction to disappear. L.J., without a word gave chase as I joined my men to assist in quelling the latest skirmish that arose.

Within a half an hour the battle was ours. We lost zero men and that meant that no families would go without fathers or husbands on this night. We gathered as much intelligence we could from the compound. The weapons and equipment we claimed would also help our cause in the long rebuilding process that would be coming. The more we searched the more we found and we knew this battle now was providing us much more than we could hope for. Before long we found the cooling bodies of Bethany and Desmond in our search of the main offices, along with a small blood trail leading out of a window which disappeared completely leading away from the building. Two things were apparent to me immediately. L.J. was certainly gone from this place although his presence could surely be felt. The other thing was that he was hurt, I only prayed not too badly. The blood we found was not significant yet still disheartening.

Upon returning to our town Jack and the rest of L.J.'s men had slipped off and we were left to rebuild Gastings even stronger than it once was. Goodbyes were not needed as we knew we would be forever linked from this day forth.

L.J. if you are out there just know you have my deepest thanks. I pledge this to you now, if you EVER need help, simply call upon Gastings and we will be at your side.

Thank You My Friend,

John Simmons.

---------------POSTED 3 HOURS LATER-------------

Hello Friends,

I am writing you all with a unexpected heavy heart. Let me explain to John and everyone else, but most importantly to you Father why I am now down a sibling. It is not out of guilt I write this Father, going there tonight I was more than prepared for death and the ramifications it held. No, tonight, surprisingly I write out of grief. Not for the loss of Bethany the person she has become. More for Bethany the potential sister I was denied due to your greed and desire for power. I mourn the person she could have been, the friend, wife, mother and sister she may have blossomed into. Most of all I mourn the daughter she could have been to you Father, not the tyrannical control monger she died as. These things that have taken place tonight and anything that happens in the future to our family, your children, can be laid at your feet. You *will* be held accountable one day Father, but for now an explanation is all I can provide.

"You have no idea just how fortunate you are Logan, you would already be long dead if Father had not instructed us otherwise", Bethany calmly stated. Upon entering her office I was slashed lightly in the arm from her dagger as she waited for me off to the side, so hearing that caught me off guard. She could have killed me true enough but still I was attacked. Although hearing that my life was being spared by my Father of all people impacted me deeper than any weapon could have. Also it was one of the first times in at least 30 years I had heard my first name spoken aloud, so that was also jarring coming from my sisters lips. Before I could ask why my Father would order something so strange, I was again set back on my guard triggered a scream of anger and fear from my sister that was followed by a loud bang. Which set into motion a series of reflexive movements so fast it would take me many moments to comprehend what had just played out.

"Desmond, fool no." was all I heard my sister bellow at her husband sneaking up behind me. At that, instinctively I ducked and turned my body toward the simultaneously occurring loud bang coming from the pistol in Desmond's hand. As I turned, my hand went to my belt where my trusted silver dagger clung to my side, my body moving quickly to the floor as my hand flung the dagger in the exact direction as the gunshot. As quick as it began the series was over and the ringing of the shot fired was still clinging in the air. I lay still on the ground for several seconds with my eyes shut tight in anticipation for the next gunshot that would assuredly end my time in this world. It never came. When I opened my eyes, I could only then process what just played out. These events I knew would change the 40 year plus game with my Family into a far more serious one.

My eyes opened and saw a flowing trail of blood coming towards me, as I let my eyes wander up I soon found them locking with my Sisters now lifeless gaze. The shot intended for me caught her directly in the heart. No matter how small a target it may have been, it was struck due to a warning she gave me. I then looked to my right side where the crumpled body of her husband Desmond now lay in the corner, my trusted battle tested dagger protruding from his chest. As the last inclinations of life twitched from his fading corpse, I realized I had to get away from this scene. It was not quiet and I knew someone may be quick to investigate. Leaving to chance if the investigating party was friendly or not was not something I was interested in doing. I quickly removed my blade and scrambled out the near open window. It was only then that I could tend to my wounded arm. Instinct alone now drove me. I doubled back to the Town, collected Jack and gave the word to his men to disperse. A word of goodbye to John was the last thing on my mind, fore I knew I had more pressing things to concern myself with.

The ride back to my home was a hectic one for me. I was now coming to grips with what had just transpired and what the meaning of these events were. First Bethany could have taken my life only to explain my Fathers wishes were to the contrary. Then before any explanations of her actions could be given, she, due to her cry of warning, simultaneously saved my life and inadvertently substituted it with her own. Now not only do I not have any of the answers I was seeking, both Bethany and Desmond lay dead, the latter directly from a flick of my wrist. I do not relish taking life, anyone's life. I do not feel I am so important in this world that I should have the power to take lives as I see fit. On a deeper note, no matter the angst she or anyone else in the Family may have caused me over the years, Bethany was still my Sister. Her death, even though not perpetrated by my hand, will stick with me for some time no doubt.....

…..... I have not forgotten about you my friend, I am glad I could be of assistance to you John and to the community of Gastings. As much as I would like to help you in the long rebuilding process your home will now go through, there are now bigger things on the horizon I must attend to. I will always be here if you need me, we are brothers in battle now. I only hope this new moniker will not lead you astray one day......

…......To you Father, I want you to know that killing anyone in this Family was never my intent, except you of course. I'm sure no doubt you are quite displeased that your daughter now lays dead, but it was by the hand of her husband not my own. You know my words can only ring with truth and it is important for you to know that I do feel loss in my heart. If for no other reason than to show you the glaring differences between the two of us. Still why would you want me alive Father? The question is haunting me, I need to know and since Bethany can no longer provide me with the answers I seek, I must turn my efforts to the rest of the Family. I can only hope it is you I next run into Father. My heart can not take the pain of killing another soul poisoned by your devious intentions. My thirst for answers will be quenched and this game will come to an end, this I promise you Father.

L.J. Stevans

----------------POSTED 1 HOUR LATER--------------

To my son L.J.,

You have made a deathly mistake, my son. The lines of war are now drawn Logan, my good graces in regards to you will no longer be afforded. Prepare for the pain of my wrath, a side of me you have not seen since the day I last laid eyes on you. After I get from you that which we I need, I will happily answer your questions.....right before I reunite you with that deceitful whore you call your Mother.

Logan Jeffery Stevans Sr.

The Chronicles of L.J. Stevans: Part 9. The Sacrifice of Jack Hundley

My Dear Friends,

After everything that has taken place over the past few weeks, I didn't think my heart could sink any lower, but I was wrong. I have had to kill a member of the Family in the form of Desmond. Even though he was mere moments from ending my own life, his death weighs heavily on me as does Bethany's. It is a shame my sister had to die in the manner she did. While it is true she was not a good person by any standards, she was my sister. I do not enjoy taking lives, it sticks to me like the most humid sweat. When I started this Chronicles it was so I could relive the past to gain a more clear picture of it and help me plan for the future. I never expected to learn the things I have, but it is done and now I can only move forward. The time for action is growing near after my latest horrid discovery this morning. After learning what I did from the sacrifice I would soon discover Jack made, I am looking to my impending confrontation with my Father and his Brother with a new anger ….a new fire....one that will only be extinguished by their final painful breath.

After the chilling letter my Father posted I knew the game had changed and since that day Jack had been acting very strangely. I now know why. Jack had been reading up anything he could find on my ancestors and being rather secret and vague. Never had he acted so in our more than 40 years of friendship. Still when he told me he had some more information to acquire I didn't give it a second thought. Why could I not see the signs, perhaps there where none to be seen because Jack wished it so. Or perhaps I just wasn't looking as hard as I should have been.

This morning I heard a faint scratching at my door, I thought it to be a stray animal that tend to visit my home from time to time. When I opened the door to find a blood covered Jack it more than set me on my heels. His face barely recognizable under the swelling and his blood soaked matted hair. There was a large gash on his left side from which blood flowed freely. Any other man would never have survived as long as he had but Jack, my best friend, my hero, a man like a Dad to me was no random person. If he was still living after all he had obviously endured, it was because he found something and his secret mission he embarked on alone was not yet over. He collapsed into my arms, his breathing was faint but his voice did not tremble and he spoke with purpose. These would be the last words he would utter aloud but not the last time I heard his voice. What he would leave me would see to that. "My Boy, listen to me" he said with focus in his Grey eyes. "Listen to the words I have recorded on this tape, it will explain all you need to know. Fight on, Logan, focus son focus, do not dwell on my death. Much still needs to be done, he cannot win......." With those words he was gone. I held him as I watched the last glimmer of light fade from his eyes.

I wanted to break down into sorrow or better yet let the rage I was feeling overtake me as I once had before. However, his last words struck home, he did this for a reason and I will not dishonor his sacrifice with hasty and pointless actions. That is when I looked down to find clutched in his hands a small recorder with a tape still in it. I will now write every word he said onto this tape. I will not change one word, on my bond and enforced by my inability to lie, everything you will now read is just the way Jack said it. If you are not one to believe in the fantastic, then you are now wasting your time reading on. Due to these words I now have a choice to make and maybe a sacrifice of my own as well. The transcription of this tape begins as such.....

.....Logan, I am sorry to have had to make this decision without you, however, after the things your Father said, I knew I must collect answers to my numerous questions. Time is short, fore I now stand in the Grand Library of your Fathers Mansion in Jacobs-town in the South, after the snowy mountain path. The location is only relevant due to the fact that I have succeeded in my quest for answers and you may need to know where it is when the time calls for it. Do not rush this place seeking revenge, word has already been sent to my men to not allow this waste of an action......Pay attention now son. I found Your Fathers journals, he has collected many over his UN-naturally long existence and it is here I found what I was looking for. I simply could not take these tomes and return because if I did then your Father would know of the things I have learned and change his time-line and plans accordingly. Or even worse, stop this knowledge from finding its way to you, and that I could not allow. This is the reason for the tape and my corresponding actions, please understand that this was the only way.

Here is what is important, your father has left you alive all these years for the simple reason that he had no other choice. You see, as we know your Father and Thomas age only one at a time but this alone could not account for their continued existence. Every generation they could only have one male child each and they must allow these boys to mature and grow to old age, they MUST allow them to live a full life........so that when the time was right they could absorb those life-forces and counter the aging process for them both, thus allowing them to go through the same routine in the next generation. The longer they let their boys live and more importantly the more they have them experience in their lives the stronger and more ripe the life-force would become. All the events in your life have been forced upon you in a sense so you could make the proverbial fruit more ripe and juicy. They use the formation of Family's and their misdeeds to drive you on your quests and eventually provide them with more fuel......

A ritual between the fathers and sons must take place where the sons must battle to their deaths.....The sons are always opposite of each other in almost every way and are drawn to one another at the right time. It says here that the sons must die in the presence of the Fathers and when the life is drawn from the sons bodies it will be absorbed into the Fathers. It says the battle is inevitable and has always taken place through countless generations. It does not say, however, that the sons had ever been privy to this information before the battle takes place and it is in this that we now have the upper hand........On the back cover you can see impressions were made on a page that had long since been removed. From what I could make out from them, it talks of a transference of immortality due to a reversal of fortunes but that is all I can make out.......

.........I know that my actions here have been detected, even I could not go unnoticed in this place, it must be due to my age boy.....ha. I am putting this tape in a secret location on my person, one I do not like to use......remember Ever-Dusk out East, and the journals we need to get past the town Militia. No one would ever look under the scalp.......those were the good old days were they not. You and I have traveled much together in these 40 years and I love you like a son. This is the last thing I can do to show that to you and offer a repayment for the many times you have saved my life over the years. This recording device will run until my last breath heed my words Logan.....Use them.........

----------------A long silence ensues until----------------------

"EVERYTHING IN QUOTES IS SPOKEN FROM MY FATHER"

........Were you expecting company Logan (My Father) or was all this for me. "I never thought you such a fool to come here Jack, in a hurry to die?" (Jack)You killed my love you vile waste of skin, Lauren's death will be avenged tonight. You might as well as forget the boy, I will find a way to kill you here and now and save L.J. The grief of murdering his own Father. "You will find that most difficult Jack, you are well past your prime and I cannot be killed at all you old sagging bag of rotting bones. Still, if you wish to try I could use the amusement, this will be fun and you shall serve as a fine penance for the death of Bethany. I will be sure to send a message to L.J. In the form of YOUR MUTILATED CORPSE".............

Grunts and the clanging of swords rang out into the ever present ear of the recorder, the battle raged for a long period only to be broken by the sound of flesh being sliced through, a groan and then......

…................”HAHAHAHAHA fool …....Oh you still live.....you are a stubborn old man......or perhaps you enjoy pain, in that case. GUARDS show this...... trespasser the error of his own stupidity and then dump him on the edge of my sons land....make him suffer.”..............

More grunts and moans of pain were all that could be heard until finally the tape ended the foul sounds that were piercing my heart.

I have lost another. Only a few times has my heart ached in this manner...Once was the day I met Jack.... The day my Mother was murdered, the day my soul first screamed with the agony of sorrow and loss. The other was........Vanessa.......never mind that for the moment however. I cannot bear this pain again, yet it seems that is my role in life. I must be the one to suffer so others do not have to. That's fair is it not? Why is it me though? Why is it my life that must be tormented in such manner? So my energy can be......*ripe* enough? Yes, real fair.

Father,

So my life was just a way for you to continue your immortal existence, is that the case? Well what if I were to just end my life here and now...You would be gone soon as well correct? Maybe this is my purpose, simply just ensure your reign will finally be at its end! It almost makes my next course of action crystal clear........but I am certainly no martyr Father. I never claimed to be, and while ending my life by my own hand would be a solution I think I have a better one. I enjoy life Father, I certainly don't want to die any time soon. Now it is clear, I can see my true reason for being and that is to continue my life another generation at the expense of YOUR immortality. I will find my cousin and figure out this.....Reversal and soon I will take into my possession the only thing you will have left....your secret to eternal life. I will not suffer forever and one day you will know the wrath of a tortured soul....Father.

Enjoy the time you have left Logan Jeffery Stevans Sr.,

L.J. Stevans.

The Chronicles of L.J. Stevans: Part 10. An Ever Changing World

Hello Friends,

Since I began these Chronicles we have discovered many things haven't we? I have..... transformed in a way right in front of you in a very short period of time, and I am sure much of this is not easy for you all to swallow. However, I know you also inhabit the same world as I and you know the.....unnatural things that are out there in the background, seemingly always just out of focus. Well I have inadvertently brought some of those things to light haven't I? My Family and their dealings are running more deeply than I have ever thought possible. And with every passing day more and more things are coming to the forefront of our minds as not only possible but dangerous. There is an immortal out there.....It even sounds funny when I say it......He is trying to continue his world draining existence with only myself and a previously unknown cousin to stand in his way or provide passage to another generation of tyranny. It must all be bewildering to you, but many of you have seen.....things..... many of you know. Even with its strange inhabitants I think it is this world in which we live that holds the most intrigue.

The unending questions you undoubtedly have about me aside for a moment. Don't you ever wonder just how we all got to this point in civilization?....I do, I think about it all the time......I wonder what came before us and why even though we live in the shadow of a mighty and technologically advanced world, are there no records of it? It is these very reasons outside of my own personal ones, that I started logging and posting these happenings in my life and our world. I do not know if the world will continue to develop and fade as it obviously once did, but if it does, I intend to leave some kind of mark for those that follow us. The same mark that should have been left for but for reasons I cannot even begin to fathom was not or has faded to a point beyond comprehension.

I think it is best that we start with what we know. We can see all around us that civilizations were here before and they were very powerful and advanced. In the larger cities, huge abandoned buildings remind us of that fact. Cars and large transport vehicles that are self powered are scattered about and some in working order. Even the horror that is fire arms, though low in number, have come back to burden us with its might. We all have come across these things and read what was said about them on the things themselves. As far as any of us can tell, it seems that the current civilization have been around and rebuilding for 200 hundred years or so. Whatever transpired here before that, happened fast and brutally. It is now common knowledge that we come from the survivors of that age past. But shockingly little information about their time is available, it's as if we were forbidden to know what transpired here around us out of some weird fear of outrage, or perhaps it was just denied to us out of shame.

Regardless of how advanced in technology our ancestors were, they obviously destroyed everything and everyone around them, but why? It has taken us many years but now larger towns are just starting to arise again. Fishing and Farming villages and tight knit communities are still the backbone of our existence, but everyday great strides are being made to help make life more....accessible to the world around us. We have these remnants of the past which, to those with the proper knowledge base has proved to be most beneficial. But why did everything fade into this? Why did the world.....reset? And most importantly can we prevent it from happening again?

It is these questions that now drive me and people of my...ilk. However it was not always that way for me. I, as many of us our in youth was originally driven by curiosity.

I always heard stories, even as a boy about these wonderful machines that could send great amounts of information from one side of the world to the other. It wasn't till I found one that I realized just how powerful a tool like this could be. That is why I choose to use this medium, that I now know to be a Global Internet Infrastructure to chronicle not only my life but the world around me. While it is no secret I do love and think very highly of myself, that I am no more important than the rest of you and it is OUR story that must be preserved. It is for that reason I was so happy to see so many of you communicating on this forum. But even with as many on here sending information back and forth as we are, there is still so little we know about our past. Will my questions ever get the answers I so desperately desire?

After everything I have lost, everything I have discovered, one person sits at the heart of most things. I now know that that same person......cannot die. How long he has lived.....that is a mystery....but he must have seen what happened here. The knowledge he has must be immense, but I know him to be a selfish and cold hearted man if a true human.... man at all anymore. He is corrupt by power now, his humanity disfigured by greed and selfishness. This man is, as you all are know privy to the fact, my father. He has taken everything from me, and I thought that finding the secret to his immortality would be enough for me but now I want to take even more from him. I want his knowledge! But in my quest for these things the question must be asked. Am I now becoming.....transformed in to the same monster as he? Will I succumb to the things that corrupted him? Have I already? I do not know the answer to these inquiries, I have never claimed to be a hero, I merely acknowledge that many of you view me as a legend of our time.....the man who cannot lie.....nothing more. As I have said many times I have done many good and bad things, I am driven by MY sense of right and wrong and that may not always align with others and I am willing to accept that.

No, I am not my Father nor will I every become him. I will help those I can, while I continue my quest for revenge and closure. I will not dishonor Jacks or my Mothers memory by rushing into a battle that is not ready to be fought let alone won. No, I will wait for my answers, wait for my time....wait for the beginning of my Fathers continued quest for life extension to reveal itself. I will wait for me to be drawn to my cousin as I was told I would be. And when that time comes and all the stars are aligned for my Father to die and for me to continue on......then I will strike.

For now, However, we can all share as much about ourselves as possible. I will continue to chronicle and continue to venture out against my Family as I see fit. They all have a part to play in this world as well as my past.....I have not forgotten this. I will also be more open to all of you about my past exploits and welcome more stories and more questions. We must continue this fore we never truly know who is watching us now or who will rediscover us in the future.

L.J. Stevans

------------------ONE HOUR LATER----------------

Who are you to request ANY information about our past? I am not your enemy L.J. But some things need to be buried where they are and forgotten. I have seen more than most and I also share.....traits with your family......You are not as unique as you may think.....You want answers....well they are out there. But the price they require and the price you are willing to pay may be two different things entirely. I suggest we meet soon, I may be able to provide you....direction......but you must be willing to sacrifice....The time for that as well as our meeting may be close at hand....Till then.....Keep your eyes open.

The Historian, Peter MacStevans.

-------------------------TWO HOURS LATER--------------

MacStevans huh??? Well just when I think I have a handle on things I am presented with an even greater mystery.

L.J. Stevans

Logan, you never have and never will you ever have a HANDLE on anything.....
MacStevans resurfaces....good now you can both die....when I allow you to stop suffering
that is. Historian, you should have stayed hidden, I will make you pay for your arrogance in
interfering in my matters yet again.

Logan Jeffery Stevans Sr.

The Chronicles of L.J. Stevans: Part. 11. A Second Chance Lost

To my Brother L.J.,

I have been reading your Chronicles on here and I have seen you basically only talk about your "great" deeds you've done. And the only people to write in have been over flattering on your character. I know you didn't kill Bethany with your own hand but in my opinion you are clearly responsible, just for the fact you got involved in our Families business yet again. You should stay out of it little brother, but at this point it doesn't really matter anyway, does it? Your fate is sealed, your death is imminent, but perhaps if you just stay out of the way you will die quickly and Father won't make you suffer to your last breath.

I have strayed off topic a bit here but you know where I'm going with this. Why don't you talk about your blood-lust and the vengeance side of you? Why don't you talk about Vanessa? Why don't you tell everyone out there about what YOU took from ME? I know how your "gift" works, once you've been asked a direct question you must answer it. So go on, tell us about your darker side. Just know this Logan, when we meet again I will be the last face you see. And I will be grinning like a school girl while watching the life fade from your eyes.

Ellen Stevans

--------------2 HOURS LATER-------------

To Ellen and everyone else reading this,

I don't really understand what your point is with all of this, after all it was YOUR actions hat led to what transpired. If you just want to hurt me by making me relive the darkest moments in my life, then fine I will oblige. I do not like talking in the narrative form, but since I am privy to all the facts of these events I will tell them as they should be told. I will hold nothing back.

The following tale is very hard for me on many different levels. While people have been killed because of my interference with their misdeeds. I had never before taken a life with my bare hands. This was also the first time I discovered that not only do some people not take advantage of a second chance you offer them, their grudge will not fade and eventually they will turn up and make you pay for your mercy.

I was about 28 years old when I decided to first sneak into one of my siblings compound, I had heard many disturbing things about Ellen so I thought I should pay her a visit. You see Ellen has never used the Families Company name as a front for her criminal activity. She didn't feel she needed to, she had most of the area locked down. Unlike some of my other sisters that paid their men in cash to buy their loyalties, Ellen used fear to control her men into servitude. She married the leader of four large town militia's, Anthony, a very clever strategist and powerful man. Even though there were the obvious benefits that came with marrying your way into a leading role of a vast army, there were never any doubts about the love they carried for one another. Even the worst kind of people are capable of unconditional love, and make no mistake about it, that's what they felt for each other. Even though they ruled the town with an iron fist, they did not kill the people in their towns nor did they tax them into poverty, while that may seem fine and dandy the residents of those outlying towns had little to no freedoms. So I felt a quick look was in order, to see if there was any help I could offer to the subjects under Ellen's rule.

I made my way into the main building on Ellen's land and as I was snooping through paper work in one of their libraries, when.......she walked in. She couldn't be more than 25 and had the face of a goddess to go with her penetrating blue-shaded-silver eyes. Even in an unflattering servants garb, her perfect figure still managed to be accented. She had long flowing dark blond lock of hair stopping just above her lower back. Quite simply, she was the most beautiful woman I have ever seen. She paused a moment as she walked in and saw me there, her first instinct was more than likely to scream but for some reason she did not. Instead she calmly closed the door and asked me who I was. Now by this age I had been with many women in fact I prided my self on my witty words and charming demeanor. Still when she addressed me my mouth got dry and for a moment I forgot my own name. I quickly gathered my self and made my introduction. "My name is L.J. Stevans" I replied. She recoiled at the mere mention of my name but still she did not flee or call out for the guards. She sat down on a box close to her and said "You're Ellen's Brother, so you're the one that has been a thorn in the side for her and her sisters. Nice to meet you, my name is Vanessa."

I almost got caught up in small talk when I realized I was breaking and entering in a very dangerous place for me to be. The door started to creak open and startled us a bit, my instincts were kicking in but hers were a tad faster and way more satisfying. She pushed me against the wall and kissed me....deeply and locked eyes with me as a signal to just go with it. Fortunately for us it was just another servant and it was clear that kissing was a standard use for this library, probably the only way most of these people had relationships. As quick as the servant entered she left closing the door quietly behind her. At that we separated our lips from one another, she had stolen my breath from me and from the look on her face I may have shook the world a bit for her as well. It was a moment we wish we could have extended, but before another word could be uttered commotion rang out in the halls. It seemed as if my presence here had been detected, I grabbed Vanessa's hand and started to lead her out towards a back exit I saw earlier, but she stopped me. "If we go together we will be found, as much as I would love to leave here perhaps this is my purpose, to help you get away. Punishment should not be so bad as I will bend the truth a bit to try and keep myself out of Jail downstairs.....GO now.....you can make it" I knew then what it was to love a lifetime in a moment. It must be that feeling which drove me to the actions I then took.

    As I have stated several times, I am no hero....not a true one anyway. I didn't want to leave her behind but I knew that if we were discovered together it would mean death for us both. I released her hand after much hesitation and we went our separate ways. I knew I could slip away rather easily, however as I got closer to the door I felt a tug at my heart strings. It was her image, I couldn't get it out of my head or my heart. So I did something I don't normally like to do, I did something foolish and heroic. I turned back but did not have to go far, fore there she was, her hands bound behind her. I could see the back of a tall man and could hear him screaming accusations at her in a voice that sounded so familiar yet I could not place it. Never the less, why wasn't she defending herself, she could have easily said hat I held her against her will, but she didn't. She just stood there stoically in defiance, but even from my vantage point I could see the tears starting to flow as they led her down to the sub floors. At that moment I knew two things for sure. First, I was not leaving this place without her, and second, I had no clue how I was going to do it. But I knew I HAD to try. To that point, I had never been in love, lust yes, but not anything close to what I was feeling right then.

    I crept down the stairs to the prison below, I heard screams which I quickly recognized as Vanessa's. They had her bound to the wall with her backside out, her top was pulled down exposing the skin on her back. I realized they were flogging her, I didn't know what to do, I usually have a plan going into these type of things, I'm not used to rescuing on the fly like this. I could not allow my mind to dwell on that, so I just sprang into action, I pulled a small yet foul smelling gas bomb I used when needing to make an escape, from my belt pouch. Without regard for my own nose I threw it just 10 feet in front of me, at the feet of the man doing the flogging. As I passed guards I pulled out my silver dagger and hamstrung them sending them to the ground in agony. I reached the jailer dishing out Vanessa's punishment, he started choking on the gas and turned to me and was greeted by my elbow crashing into his nose, he staggered back but did not fall. I lunged at him with a second attack, this time a swift kick to the groin followed by a brutal knee right under his chin. This time it put him on his back and it was at that moment I knew why I recalled that voice. It was William, the man responsible for the crimes in Milton just 5 short years before that was staring back at me with instant recognition in his eyes. He tried to make his way to his feet but was met with one of mine to his head instead. I pulled Vanessa's shirt back on to her and cut her down, she had tears in her eyes as she fell into my arms. Even through all that she was still the most beautiful creature I had ever come across, I almost got lost into her eyes again, but the putrid smell creeping up to me prevented that. We ran back past the guards and up the stairs we climbed. All the commotion had settled down up stairs, so getting out was not that difficult. The smell left us soon, however the ramifications of these actions would linger for much longer.

Jack was waiting by the south wall just as we planned before hand, we found an old truck weeks back and got it running for this mission, simply because horses would be far to slow if things went bad. I'm very glad we decided to bring the vehicle because bad is exactly how it went. He opened the door and gave me a perplexed look when I slid Vanessa over to him. "You just have a woman magnet strapped to you somewhere don't you Logan" He quipped. "Just hit the gas old man" I replied to him with laughter under my words. Vanessa had passed out by this time and as we drove away from the frenzy I started, I couldn't help but once again get lost in her beauty, this time I didn't hold myself from it.

We couldn't return to my property, William saw me, so by now Ellen knows everything, and soon they will be coming for me. We stopped at one of Jack's many safe houses, the man was very connected. I gently put Vanessa on a bed in the back room and started to treat her wounds, the pain eventually woke her. She opened her eyes and looked up at me, at first with confusion, but after I held up the gauze and gave her a disarming smile, she nodded her head with understanding. At that she closed her eyes again, this time knowing I was there watching over her. She awoke sometime later and I explained to her everything, why I was there, the situation with my Family even the events in Milton with William. I asked her why he was there, and she told me he was the head guardsman and jailer, and that he also was one of most skilled trackers in the region. She made sure to emphasize that, knowing he would be on our trail soon.

As we ate dinner that night with Jack, she told us all about herself, she was an only child and at the age of 15 she was sold to Ellen by her parents. Human trafficking was rare in our region but still did happen, but I felt an immediate bond with her, she was like me.....abandoned by her family, cast aside like an after thought. Jack left soon after dinner to obtain information about any movement on Williams or my Families part. Once he left I knew Vanessa was going to ask me a question, one that I knew I would have to answer truthfully, and likely embarrass myself.

"Logan, why did come back for me?" She asked. There it was, my mind started a long structure of words about her beauty and how she made me feel, but my heart intervened and forced my lips to utter "Because I love you" with hardly a hesitation. My face reddened as I waited for her imminent laughter. It never came, when I looked back at her, she had tears in her eyes again but not in pain or sadness this time, but in realization. Realization in not only did she know I meant what I had just said but that she felt the same way for me. She took my hand in hers and I slowly brought it up to her face, she nestled into it and stared into my eyes as she returned the phrase to me. I leaned forward slightly and kissed her. With that we fell into one another completely body, mind and soul. I have had sex with a few women at that point, but with Vanessa it was the first time I had ever made love.

When we awoke, I checked her wounds and bandages and we sat down to eat. Almost from the moment we left the bed we could not stop holding each others hand, We sat that way throughout breakfast as we talked about what was next. I coyly asked if she had any friends or anywhere safe she could go, but the smile on my face betrayed my words, fore we both knew we were never to part again if it could be helped. So with Jacks help we ran. I had never done that before. Jack once said to me during our search for safety that standing up and fighting for the one you love is one thing. But to run with the one you love....now that is a true test of emotions.

For the next 2 years we were on the move, never in one place more than 3 months at most. However, we never got close to running into trouble, thanks to Jack and his connections. Jack's informants also let us know it was indeed the head guardsmen that was on our trail. Still, we always stayed 3 steps ahead of William, but to his credit he never stopped searching.

During our time together, Vanessa and I lived like tourists. We never laid down roots, kept moving, seeing all the wonders our world has to offer. It remained that way, until we thought we may be safe in this last town we found called Elders Creek over on the coast by The Great Eastern Ocean. We were isolated, close enough to the town to stay well supplied but still far enough away to ensure our protection. Even Jack, who frequently checked in on us thought we were safe. We found out 3 months prior, that Vanessa was with child and I was to be a Father. So we wanted to set up a home....and we did. Deep down I felt that it was just a matter of time until we were found, because even though you stop running the ones searching for you only heighten their pursuit. And heighten his pursuit William did.

A few months had passed with no sign that our trail had been picked up. Jack and I were returning from a mission close by, helping run off some highwaymen, and when we reached the edge of my land Jack and I parted ways for the night. As I.......(L.J. Pauses and takes a deep breath and wiped his eyes).....As I returned home I could not have foreseen the horrible sights that would befall upon my eyes. When I opened the door a strong scent of blood hung in the air, I looked down and saw that I was standing in a puddle of it, I let my eyes raise up and saw a trail leading up the stairs and down the hall. I followed the path of blood to my study, I opened the door slowly, my brain already knowing what I would find even though my heart held out hope. As soon as I stepped over the doorway my eyes went straight to a table, on the table lay Vanessa, my wife. my love, my soul mate. She was butchered like cattle the only thing not mutilated or covered with blood was her head, it sat on the front of the table eyes open, fear and dread caught frozen forever. I dropped to my knees sobbing, for what it felt like an eternity, but my tears quickly began growing to rage, a rage I had never felt before. Small at first, as most flames are, it soon had me shaking in place as if my body could not hold the emotion building within me. Something caught my eye then, I looked down on the floor and noticed that there were several trails of blood and in fact they spelled out something. I reached up and turned on the light and read the cold words written in my dead wives blood. It said "This time you WILL burn". I barely had time to read it when the room erupted in flames that seemed to mimic what I was feeling in my heart. It seemed this nightmare may be short lived fore I, in my grief had walked into a fire trap.

Even over the roar of the fire I could hear taunts and yelling outside led by a voice I recognized at once. The rage was now uncontrollable and it likely is the only thing that would free me from that hellish room. Without a care for my own safety, I grabbed the closest chair and ran straight towards and out the window. I plunged a good 13 feet to the ground but was up in a flash, rage, vengeance and adrenaline fueling me now. I looked at the now quieted men in front of me. I must have looked like a demon to them, in fact I think the back of my clothing may have been literally on fire. The stunned men gathered themselves quickly and looked to William for their next orders. He motioned for them to attack, to my great joy and anticipation they obeyed.

The first 2 men came at me weapons drawn, from the right side of my belt I pulled my single shot pistol and dropped the closest man on the right. On my left side of my belt I produced my trusty silver dagger and I threw it with all my force, taking the second man down with head shot. I was running now, making a bee line towards the 3 remaining men, I grabbed my dagger from the skull of the dead guard as I past him. I could see the panic in Williams eyes. He pushed both men forward and ordered the one with a gun to fire, flustered he hastily did so, nailing me in the left shoulder, had he not been in such a fear stricken state I more than likely would have been stopped in my tracks then and there. But fear and adrenaline can do amazing things, for him it turned him into a boy firing a weapon clumsily at a demon he helped create. For me it fueled me forward and turning a hard shot into a wound I could not even feel.

Before he could get another shot off, my dagger was plunged into his heart. I stopped and let the now charging final guard close the distance, I retrieved my dagger once again and pulled the dead guardsmen sword from his sheath. I characteristically am not a fantastic swordsmen, however I am proficient enough to make a name for my self in the tournament circles,.I would visit them whenever I was too bored or short on coin. None of that mattered though, because when you are running on the type of rage I was, skill hardly mattered. I fought as if I did not care about living because in this case I didn't. He got no closer than 2 steps to me before I dispatched him with a brutal slice of my sword that caught him in the neck. I pushed him off my blade and let my eyes focus on William. A smile crept on my lips as I realized the same thing he was now noticing. After all the chaos and death it was now only two of us.

I stared at him as if I was shooting blades from my eyes, he had a look of reality on his face. Any thoughts I may have had of him being paralyzed by the totality and consequences of his action quickly faded from my mind. He was not that type of man, he did not care about what he had done and I now understood that in some sick way this is exactly what he wanted all along. This became more apparent to me as I stepped forward to him, his expression changed to a deranged snarl, one that showed his devious thoughts. The snarl became more of a smile of amusement and mirth as he simultaneously gathered his emotions and pulled his pistol out from behind his back. No words were spoken yet as I began lumbering towards him, I never stopped coming even as he fired, his shot hit me right in my upper left chest. To my amazement it dropped me to the ground and this time I most certainly felt the impact.

Sensing the end was near he started at me again, this time caught up in his own arrogance he dropped his pistol and drew a sword. He was mocking me now but his beaming was cut short when he noticed that I was somehow beginning to rise yet again. His visage turned to disbelief, he had no clue just how deep my fury ran. My breathing was labored now I could feel fatigue, injuries and quite possibly death starting to creep in my heart and mind. As the pattern for me has kept repeating in my life in times of peril my instincts and strategic acuity kicked in. Thinking tactically now I threw my dagger at him as hard as I could, visibly showing him the strain and effort behind the toss. Expectantly, he parried it perfectly to the ground as I knew and anticipated he would. Feeling in control now that the taunts started once again, why wouldn't they. I was hurt and it was no secret that William is one of the best swordsmen in the region. To him the battle was over.

Brashly he explained to me that all his men had there way with Vanessa and they made her feel every millisecond of her death. He continued on boasting about the fact that he himself drove his sword into her stomach and through her womb so there was no way my legacy would be carried on. Deciding that now was my most opportunistic moment I allowed that vile comment to be the basis of my plan. I allowed pain and anger to yet again show on my face and with that I ran at him, presumably with reckless abandon. I lead with a short sword I picked up off the ground as I returned to me feet. I screamed and held out my sword wide to my left, but as he moved to block my attack I sprung my true intentions into motion. I stopped short and and nailed him right between the eyes with a good sized rock I managed to palm. He stumbled back and dropped his sword, I deftly went into a roll and retrieved my dagger from the earth where I had him place for me and deposited directly into Williams throat. He understood now that while he may have had the advantage, *I* had the plan. I stood there watching him slowly accept what had just transpired as he died. For the first and only time in my life I absorbed every moment of a mans death with glee, zero remorse and to be honest with great satisfaction. Any inkling of my Fathers nature passed on to me may have escaped onto my face and in my heart at that moment, to this day, I don't mind.

Jack arrived moments later and found me there sitting soaking in my own blood, my burning house served as a dramatic background I would venture to guess. He started to walk towards me, while he stopped quickly to search Williams body, ever the detective. As he did so he explained that he saw the smoke from the fire and came as fast as he could. He stopped his words short when he saw my crumpled form shaking with anger and sorrow. It was then when I looked up and saw Jacks face that I truly lost myself to grief. My sobbing became an uncontrollable river of pain and loss. This was the first time Jack had ever seen me cry. Not even when he arrested my Father for my Mothers murder did I shed a tear. He knew the gravity of what happened to me but even so, he knew time was short and he had to get me going. He explained to me that more men were on the way, to which I coldly responded "Let them come, Hell will be overflowing tonight no doubt". Neither one of us knew exactly what I meant but at least it sounded good. Not allowing me to succumb to my grief he grabbed me by my good arm, picked me up and said. "Your not going to let them win now? Are you Logan? After all that they have taken from you, your just going to sit there and die? Get up Boy." So up I went. I was fueled and carried as much by his words as I was by Jack's shoulder as we moved to his truck. I had never been as hurt or exhausted as I was in that moment. My heart was heavy and more racked with sorrow than my body was with pain. I did not know how badly I was truly hurt but at the time I didn't care. Revenge and my own death was the only things I wanted then. William may have been dead but it went deeper than him. After I had my vengeance then I could die, at least I would be back with her....my love.

As much as I may have wanted to in that moment I knew that I could not really be giving up as easily as I was contemplating. Even after this sorrow was to be bearable my life had to continue. So much was left for me to put right, even if I didn't want to accept it just then. As we drove away I looked back at my burning house and thought of Vanessa again, I thought of everything that had happened not only in the last hour but the last few years really.... but soon I thought of nothing as my world would quickly begin fading to black as my body would finally start to give. As it did I came to the decision of what would be next for me and what I would need to keep going.

A week later I regained full consciousness, I opened my eyes and saw that I was in a small clinic, Jack was asleep by my bed. I moved my arm around and was relieved that there was not too much pain, as soon as I felt I was ready and able, I started moving and I knew I had to move fast. When Jack opened his eyes I was gone and so were my clothes and weapons. He knew where I was headed to, and decided to give me a 30 minute head start before he came after me. After all, he can't be held responsible for something he was not present for. At least that is what he would tell me later......

…..............Excuse me for a moment would you..........

----------------10 MINUTES LATER AFTER REGAINING HIMSELF-------------

…...Sorry for that, I had to step away to gather myself....

I found the fastest transportation I could, in this case it was a truck...Jack's truck to be exact. I kind of stole it, and made a bee line for Ellen's compound. I once again had no trouble sneaking in, and once I did I didn't care about being detected anymore. Men rushed me and as they did they fell before my feet. I sent many men to Hell on that day, fury burning in my eyes. I walked in to the section where Ellen and Anthony stayed. Ellen stood up as did Anthony, he came in front of me in defiance saying he would not allow me to kill Ellen. I got even closer to him and told him in a whisper, "I'm not here for Ellen". With those words I plunged 2 daggers into his chest and stomach one from each hand, I looked him in the eyes and saw the disbelief that sunk in. Then I turned my gaze to my Sister and as I did I pulled both daggers across his abdomen in opposite directions, opening him wide onto the marble floor under our feet.

Ellen was frozen by fear as I walked closer to her, she made no movement, a look of dread now occupied her face. I told her this, as I now stood in front of her. "You took my love away and now I took yours, not an even trade by a long shot but it will have to do. I am letting you live because I can't bring myself to kill you even now. But more than that I am not like you and the rest of our family, I am a man of second chances. I gave William one 5 years ago in Milton, and it burned me didn't it? He chose to stay with the family and continue his criminal ways, so I had to revoke that chance. Do not squander this second chance I'm granting YOU sister. If we meet again and you are still with the Family doing fathers bidding...plain and simple I will end you." And with that I walked out.....she made no move against me.

In fact today's post was the first I had heard from her since that day. It seems by her words that she has stretched that second chance as far as it could go. Another revocation may be in order. But that is work for another day.

I was not sure if I should discuss Vanessa. It may have been years ago but it still hurts to this very day. I gave second chances to many people...many people indeed but not to myself not to my heart. That part of my heart that loves the way it did when I was with Vanessa died with her I believe. Perhaps one day it can be awaken from the recesses of my shattered soul.

55

I know I rambled on here for a long bit, but I felt you needed the entire story, but now I must think on recent events, you will hear from me soon everyone. Stay Safe out there.

L.J. Stevans

The Chronicles of L.J. Stevans: Part 12. The Immortal Story of Fathers and Sons

To L.J. And the World,

Some stories in this world are better left untold, I have always believed in this statement. The world at large is not ready for the truth of how the previous age destroyed itself. I and others like me have always hoped that humanity, if given the chance will make the correct decisions without the guiding hand of a historical record. What good would it do if all the answers in life were just handed to you? For countless ages history was recorded and past down through generations, but it did nothing to prevent the patterns or war, greed and selfish destruction. This age, however has not had that benefit of history to blueprint mans journey, and look how far you all have come. Civilization has stayed small but strong, hard work has been what the majority of you have depended on. I know that the evils that plagued the past are still prevalent in this day and age, but never has it been so openly opposed.

My name is Peter MacStevans. Over the many years of my life I have been referred to as many things, Watcher, Keeper, Protector but I think I like Historian the most. It is the most accurate description of who I am. I keep the records of the world, I have done so for countless years and I will continue to do so for countless more. As you now know there are Immortals living amongst you, which is another thing that makes your generation unique. You are the first group in history that has flat out known that we walk beside you. Obviously there have been myths and legends, but with the secret being reveled by your Mother, L.J. and then confirmed by your Father. Mankind is privy to something they have never been before. So there really is no point in trying to hide the fact that I am also Immortal.

We are not so small a number either, by my last count there are still 98 Immortals out there. Some of you may wonder how do I know this. My resources for gathering such and all information is.....great to say the least. Most of the information I get is from you out there. Other means of fact gathering however, fit into the category of ...... unconventional and beyond the reach of mortal men. All but two of us are original, meaning we were born this way, and truth be told, "born" is not the correct term exactly. We never aged one day in our lives, we were never babies, we didn't "grow up" so to speak. No. We were.... put here this way, just as we are. By whom? You may ask. And to that question not even I know the answer to.

Nonetheless, all of us, save two, were created this way. Care to take a guess as to whom those two would be. Ah yes....now you see my point L.J., and this is the story I wish to share with you today.

Long ago before years and numbers even had meaning, there were exactly 200 of us here and we were restricted to a place on this Planet that no longer exists. We watched as man was born and developed into what it has become. Some of us even desired to be worshiped by your kind, others didn't feel you were worthy to worship us. Over time those who fit into those two extreme groups warred with one another, and eventually our numbers were more than cut in half by the constant battling. 98 original Immortals were all that survived, in fact all but two of the 98 didn't even fight at all. The two remaining Immortals that took part in the war were a pair of twin brothers Fel and Kel. They fought on opposite sides of the war and injured each other brutally during the fighting. They were so badly hurt that they knew they would not survive long in the world apart. So the brothers reconciled their differences and found exile in a cave in an, at one point unknown and yet to be discovered region. It seemed as though Fel and Kel did this to live in harmony with each other in hopes that one day they would recover and rejoin their true family. Well at least one of them believed that to be the case.

Fel was the one that talked Kel into the idea of exile and peace, but in truth this was a cunning ruse by Fel. Fore he knew something Kel did not. If he were to kill Kel and take his life force, his Immortality would be regained in full. Kel was not aware of these facts so you can imagine his shock when his brother impaled him on a spiked stalagmite on the cave floor. Kel still lived for a time just as Fel had planned. He knew he needed to absorb his brothers essence while he still drew breath. Kel now realized what was happening and knew what was to come next. His quick thinking cost Fel his chance. Just as Kel's energy was being absorbed by Fel, Kel placed his hands above him on the stalagmite and drove himself down farther with all of his force. Which ended not only his suffering but his brothers chance at survival. Fel remained there for centuries slowly decaying from his battle wounds. Stories by this time were being told all through out humanity but still our presence here was nothing more than a strong rumor, as was the location of one who could grant immortality to a brave and adventurous mortal. However, as with most myths and legends, there are always those that would chase after them.

Over time people would talk about venturing out to try to gain immortality from the speculated host, some even claimed to have been close to finding the location of Fel's cave. Until one day 700 years ago, two brothers managed to separate fact from fiction and locate the tomb. Upon uncovering the cave these brothers found Fel on the floor in agony and decaying, but neither man knew how to obtain Fel's gift. After all his years of suffering, Fel was ready to move on. However, Fel being the ever vengeful person he was decided to pass the brothers a curse along with the gift they came for. The curse you see, was that the brothers would age but only one at a time. During each generation or "lifespan" they would have to Father one male child each. Making it even more difficult, these boys would have to be born under the same moon. If the two men wanted to extend their eternal lives they would have to force the boys into long, full and emotional lives and then into battle just as Kel and Fel did. After, as their sons lay weakened and close to death, they would take the life forces of their children into their own. The names of the twin brothers that uncovered the location of Fel's cave were Logan and Thomas MacStevans.....my human born sons.

For years I watched them use this curse to sustain life without even a hint of remorse, as time went by they even turned it into a game. As men they were not evil but the curse of the brothers Fel and Kel turned them into beasts. Beasts that would become humanities biggest drain. Now their power is greater than ever, if left unchecked their power mongering will tip humanity into another tail spin, from which it may never recover.

I never intended to reveal this to the world, alas never before have one of their sons been as extraordinary as you seem to be L.J.. You can break this cycle and your reward would be to join our ranks of the Immortals. How you can achieve this however, is something you will have to figure out for yourself. I only ask one thing of you, do not be tempted in the same ways your Father and Uncle were. It takes two to carry the gift and the curse but only one to enjoy the benefits of immortality without the burdens of Fel's curse. This one can be the beacon of guidance humanity has waited for. You have the potential to be that beacon.

That is all the information I will provide you and you should feel proud to even have gotten that. I have not spoken to a mortal in quite a long time. Seek your answers in the world around you Logan, fore if you look hard enough you will discover the truth and the secret of the Immortals.

Peter MacStevans, Historian

The Chronicles of L.J. Stevans: Part 13. The Hero He Was Meant To Be

Hello World,

My my, we have had an exciting time recently haven't we? Life was so much easier when I just broke up crime organizations or got shot at or have my house burned down. I never thought I would long for those days back. I am now caught in this self propelled machine of chaos, that I apparently kick started. I knew the origins of myself and my Father were.....complicated, but this. This is even more than I bargained for. I never knew asking questions could bring about so much trouble, nor could I ever conceive just how deep my Fathers evil streak went.

I had to grow up very fast because of the actions my Father perpetrated, and I excepted that. It was simple. Dad marries Mom. Mom finds out Dad is psychotic. Mom turns to the law for help. Officer falls in love with Mom. Mom then murdered by Father. Father goes to jail. Son cast out looking for answers. See easy, nothing to complex there, never did I think the next line would go as such. Son finds out Dad is Immortal and reason for all turmoil in the world. Son must now kill Dad and his Twin to take Immortality for himself. You see, right there that's what I'm saying. I didn't sign up for all this insanity. I am not a hero!!! I'm not!!!! I don't want this. I am just a man. One that was wronged. I want vengeance not justice!!!

…..OK perhaps I help the surrounding world when I can. Perhaps I stick my neck out for the occasional teenager bound to be fire-bombed. Still I'm just a man!!! A man that rights wrongs where he sees them. One that will try to free others from servitude and fall in love with them. One that can love so intensely that when that love is taken will turn into a demon of rage to avenge the loss. See I'm still a man. A normal flawed man. Alright maybe not....normal....just a man that was born without the ability to lie. A man that is seeking revenge for the crimes against him and others......

…...Oh...I see now, ha ha. This was never easy, never cut and dry, because *I* along my nature was never simple. Maybe I'm not normal or everyday. Perhaps I lived this way because I was supposed to. Perhaps I just fought against who I really was......Perhaps I thought by denying my destiny I could be free of it.....is that what I want? To be free of it? Or to just believe that I am? I think I get it now. Being flawed and striving for normalcy is what I'm supposed to strive for.

When I first began these Chronicles I asked you all a question. I asked. What is "Greatness"? Remember that? Maybe "Greatness" is simply realizing that there is NO denying who you are. It could be that "Greatness" is finally standing firm and living the life you were meant to. My bloodline on both sides of my Family is full of potential, and I feel it may be time to live up to it. It's time to take the fight to the Family itself. It's time to show the world just who I am and who I can become. Prepare yourselves Family, as should you Father, because the time for action is drawing near. No more fear of what I can lose, because simply waiting for the end feels worse than losing. Jack made me swear I would wait for the right time, and I did. But I never said that I wouldn't try and move the timetable forward.

Cousin!!! It is time we meet. Friends it is time for favors to be called in. Do not be surprised when I come to you for assistance. The world is in greater danger than ever and we all missed it, so indeed it is time to become one unit and fight back. It is time for my Father to die. It's
time the Family becomes no more. I will wait for you cousin but as I do I will take the fight to the Family. It will all end here in this generation. For no other reason than it is time. But most of all it is long past time that I become the *Hero* I never wanted to be.

L.J. Stevans

The Chronicles of L.J. Stevans: Part 14. A Declaration of War / A Gift

L.J.,

So you think you are a Hero now do you son? After all your years of sneaking around and back fighting, now you want to be a man? I find it funny that the Historian's little pep talk fired you up so much. Once I get what I need from you I will take care of that old man as well. After thinking things out I have come to a few decisions. First, I don't need you in perfect health to drain you of you life force. In fact, the closer to death you are the easier it will be for me. Also I think you are right, it is time for you to meet your cousin, in fact he and Ellen are outside of your house right now with a few friends of theirs. They are just awaiting my signal to attack, once you're beaten within an inch from death they will bring your broken body to me. Because of your non stop actions, I just want this to be over, you have lived quite long enough my son. Enough of the games, play time is finished. I have dispatched my men to go make examples out of a couple of towns that may be of interest to you. So wave goodbye to Milton and Gastings, they will soon lay in ruins just to ensure no one will ever think to oppose me again. You wanted a war so I will bring you a war... I will see you very soon.

Logan Jeffery Stevans Sr.

--------------------6 MONTHS LATER----------------

Hello friends,

I know it has been quite some time since you last heard from me. Now that it is safe to come back the the Chronicles, I have quite the tale to tell today. Much has happened in the past 6 months, most of it has been a blur. In this time I have lost some friends but also gained important allies. Gastings, the old fishing village I once helped save, indeed was burned to the ground. Fortunately I was able to send word ahead and get as many people out of there before hand as possible. Before I get to far ahead of myself I want to take you back 6 months, because that is when the face of this war as well as I changed forever once again.

I had just read my Fathers latest threat, when I heard noises coming from outside. Not wanting to be ambushed, I decided to make my stand in my study, where I already was. There was only one way in or out here. I knew if I could force them through this one doorway, I might stand a chance or at least take as many down with me as I could. I was expecting to be rushed by a flood of guardsmen. So you could imagine my surprise when it was a lone man I had never seen before that came at me.

He stood right in the doorway, a brash look of ease swept across his face. I stood waiting and ready for an attack, when he began to speak. "Hello Cousin" He calmly stated. "I would like to introduce myself, I am Mathew, I have looked to this day with anticipation for a very long time. Now that the pleasantries are out of the way, you have a choice Logan, either walk out of here with me and make it easy on everybody. Or I swear to you I will make you suffer to the bitter end." He smirked as he continued on. "You see cousin, I saw what you wrote and your words intrigued me, not because I wish to help you...ha-ha-ha. Heavens no, but because I figured it out Logan, the secret. I know how to master this curse our Fathers have brought on themselves as well as us, and more importantly I know how to take it for myself." He now had my full attention.

"It was so easy, it only takes one, Logan. More to the point, me. You see here is how it goes, I kill you and take your life force, then it's as simple as turning our Fathers against one another. Just like the Immortal brothers they stole this gift from." He boasted as if it were all just a formality. He started to talk once again but was knocked down from a backhand that neither one of us saw coming. Mathew rubbed the side of his face as he looked up with surprise to see his Fathers standing over him. I took a step back as Thomas looked down at his son. "So, that is your plan is it?" He began "You think you can betray me and get away with it? You don't really think I would let you off your leash to plot against me do you boy? Now get up and do what you were ordered to do, I want him hurt not dead Mathew." He managed to yell, but you could see he breathed heavy now, every move seemed to drain him. Time was certainly not his ally and at this point you could tell it was he who was in the aging cycle of the curse. His skin was wrinkled and loose on his bones, there was nothing but a few white hairs left on his head, his eyes looked sunken, completely tired and haggard as did his full expression. Still after that blow he just delivered to his son, I knew not to underestimate him.

My uncle never said a word to me, in fact all talking had ceased as Mathew pulled his saber and sword from his belt and started at me. I pulled my silver dagger to compliment my short sword. He went to work immediately bringing in his sword high to my left. I ducked under it and went into a roll, bringing both dagger and sword up and in close to his chest. He blocked both weapons out wide and countered with his saber just missing my arm. I came back at him with a kick followed by 2 successive high/low cuts one catching a small area on his leg. He disengaged at that and stepped back to check the wound, but after I drew first blood the last thing I was going to do was let his get his rhythm back. I ran at him, launching my dagger at him as I have so many times in battle, however this time I pulled up short. In fact it was an abrupt halt, my mind was baffled and I'm sure I wore a look of total disbelief at the moment. I was not sure what I would do next as he seemingly with little effort plucked my blade from mid air with his bare hands, it was at that moment when I realized that I was in a great deal of trouble.

He tossed my dagger aside and looked at it as if was a toy, he then turned his attention back to me and laughed to himself. I was now starting to panic. There was no question he was much a better fighter than I was, I could only hope that I was the more cunning. Either way I knew that now it was all or nothing. I could not afford to let him attack again, I needed to catch him off guard. So I did what any rational man would do in my place, I ripped my shirt off and ran at him screaming bloody murder. A look of utter amusement with a hint of confusion came over him. He brought is saber straight out at me, I knew this was my only chance. I would have to try something dangerous and stupid, it was my last hope and it turned out to be the beginning of a sequence of events that would change the entire course of my life.

My left shoulder has been wounded many times in my life, I told you all before that I was shot in it in the aftermath of Vanessa's death. There were also many other times I have yet to disclose to you that the area had been wounded. It's as if my arm has a magnet in it or something. As much as it hurt the first few times it was injured, the pain was well worth it, because on this occasion it would serve me as an asset. I rushed him, screaming as loud as I could, he had his saber out in front of him and I simply ran my left shoulder into it. He was completely confused now, coming close to flat out asking me why I would do something so reckless no doubt. However I knew something he didn't quite yet understand, I brought my sword up and slashed at his left arm, forcing him to block out wide, he knocked the sword from my hand as he did. That is when I made my move. He couldn't bring his saber out to help because it was trapped in my shoulder, I twisted my body to my left giving him no choice but to lose control of the saber. He swept his sword at me from left to right clearly thinking this was the killing blow, I had other plans however. I stretched my shirt out as I turned and and wrapped up his sword within it. I disarmed him and grabbed the sword by the hilt while completing my turn, while doing so I thrust it out forward with all the strength I could muster. At that it was done, our eyes locked, I could clearly see the flabbergasted gaze my cousin now wore. He brought his stare down from my eyes to the sword that was now protruding from his chest.

Without a second thought, I turned again, this time pulling the saber out of my shoulder as I made a 180 turn to face my uncle. Who was now storming towards me with a look of pain and anger on his face that I recognized oh so well. Finishing my turn I threw the saber at him with everything I had left. It was a hit. However, with him being Immortal I knew this would only buy me a few moments, but moments I desperately needed to figure out my escape. I started to plan my getaway, but suddenly stopped as I watched him fall to the ground, to my amazement he did not and would never get up again. I waited a few long moments to see if he was truly dead. Then to my surprise a light glow started emanating from the wound, I had no idea what this meant. Lord knew I had no idea what I was to do next. It was then that I noticed I was not alone in the room any longer.

An elder white haired man now stared at me from across the room, how he got there was beyond me. I hardly cared anymore, I knew I could not win another battle right now, the last sequence of events left me completely drained. The man walked over to Thomas, placed his hand over the glowing spot from his wound and grabbed it. He then turned to me and held it out in front of him and said. " Take this, Grandson" The words nearly knocked me over, but he continued. "This is a reward for stopping at least one of them before any more damage could be done." I realized now that I was in the presence of The Historian, Peter MacStevans. "How did I kill him?" I asked. "Aside from the hands of another Immortal, there was only one other way to kill one of us. The blood of the brothers son, it was your blood that could kill Thomas. Just as it is only Mathew's that can kill your Father, Logan. But you already knew that, didn't you?" I humbly replied. "Not exactly knew, but I felt it was my only shot, my last shot actually."

He now walked towards me and started to hand me the light as he spoke. "Take this gift Logan, you cannot defeat your Father in your present condition, and I fear that after tonight's events, he will be very difficult to locate. It may take years to find him again. Years that quite frankly you don't have." "What do you mean? Are you granting me Immortality?" I carefully asked. He laughed at that and responded. "No Logan, Immortality can not be given from just one brother. It is a split curse, remember? As you can tell, Thomas was the one aging, so while you cannot gain Immortality from him you can have the part of the curse that was plaguing him. He has been aging for 30 years and it is those 30 years I can grant you from his energy. You need this time to complete the mission I have bestowed upon you, without this gift you will surely die long before you have a chance to finish what you began."

My mind worked quickly to try and comprehend everything that just played out before me. Tonight was a close call, too close. My advancing age is starting to hinder my reflexes amongst other things, and I knew what my Grandfather was saying to be the truth. Without another thought I stepped in front of The Historian. He placed the light to my chest and held it there, I looked down at the light, then back to the old sages face and then there was nothing left for me.... but darkness.

I awoke in a vehicle, a large one, I believe it was once used for transporting large amounts of products. I started to sit up and wipe the grogginess from my eyes, when I noticed my hands. I now had hands removed of liver spots and age. As I sat up I did so with no pain from old tired bones. I was young, if The Historian was right then that means I am now once again 24. I was astounded to say the least. But before I got too far ahead of myself, I had to figure out just where I was. I looked up to the drivers seat and saw a woman there, I simply uttered the word stop. She quickly pulled the Van off to the side of the road, turned it off and spun around to me. "Who are you? And what have you done with L.J. Stevans?" She asked impatiently. "I am L.J. Stevans, and just whom might you be? I responded. "You?...You can't be L.J., he is over 50 years old." she spat back at me."Yes, I know it is difficult to understand but I am in fact L.J., I was just....well honestly I don't know how to explain it ye..." I was cut off mid sentence as she hurriedly interrupted me. "You figured it out, the curse I mean" She excitedly stated. "What, wait just who are you and how do you know so much?" I asked, now clearly frustrated. "Oh, sorry how rude of me, I'm a friend, I'm here to help. My name is Rebecca...Rebecca Hundley, I'm Jacks daughter.....

.......With that I must stop here friends I have many things that need attending to, but I will be back soon fore there is much more to tell.

L.J. Stevans

The Chronicles of L.J. Stevans: Part 15. Rebecca Hundley

Hello Once Again Friends,

Much has happened over the last six months, first the town of Gastings has been completely destroyed. However, we were able to send warning so they didn't loose many people in the razing of the small fishing village. At the request of the men of Gastings, the families, being women and children have been sent to a safe, private and fairly secret location. This allowed the 120 or so men to ride with us. We needed numbers for this upcoming war, Gastings was the first town to provide us with some. I appointed John Simmons to lead and look after these men, fore I am not a micro-manager, truth be told I'm not much of a General either, but desperate times...right.

My Uncle Thomas and Cousin Mathew are now dead as you know, both of them by my hand. It's kind of funny when you think about, there is such little trust among the Family, that Thomas followed and basically spied on his own son. For doing so, he lost his life along with his sons. Whenever I have taken the life of a Family member, it has been met with a tirade laden post from my Father. This time there was nothing but silence, which truth be told scares me even more. Just as the Historian predicted, my Father has gone under ground and into hiding, I don't know what he is planning but I would be a fool if I took this action by him and wrote it off as a weakness. My Father may be a lot of things but weak is certainly not one of them.

OH yeah, how could I forget. I am 30 years younger now! This is by far the craziest thing to happen to me yet. My Grandfather...The Historian, gave me this gift for stopping my Cousin and Uncle. He said I wouldn't be able to finish my mission without more time. I am now starting to come to grips with all of this. Don't get me wrong, I don't miss the aching body, the tired and sore back, the weakness, along with everything else that comes with age. I especially don't miss the regressing reflexes and agility. Still this is all a bit much to take in all at once. I always knew there were "strange" things out in the world, but this, this pushes the limit of "strange".

Yet another one of my houses has been burned to the ground, I really liked this one too. I know there are a lot of bigger, more important and dangerous things going on around me right now. But I would like to take a quick moment to pay respects to my fallen houses.......OK, now I feel better. All joking aside, I lost everything I had in regards to Vanessa, along with countless other irreplaceable items but I guess it was time to start anew. I am sure many of you are wondering how I made it out of the fire alive. Well that leads me into an introduction.

To best accomplish that, I must take you back to the end of my last post.....

…..”I am Rebecca Hundley, Jack's Daughter.” That one sentence she said to me almost knocked me over. She went on to explain to me that 25 years ago, on one of his routine informant checks, Jack met a women and he was quite enamored with her. He started seeing her as often as he could and, well to make a long story short, it turns out that even at his age at the time, a child was not out of the question. I was now talking to he proof of that fact. At this point I would like to hand the story over to Rebecca, she can tell her tail much better than I can.

-------------REBECCA SITS DOWN---------------

Hello world,

As L.J. said, I am Rebecca Hundley-Stevans. Before you start asking about that last addition to my name let me catch you all up on how everything happened. Over the years my Father would come to my town quite often, sometimes 4-5 times a month. When he did he would bring money to help my mom, as well as finding time to teach me a new skill. When I was old enough he told me everything about what he did. After some time he made me promise that if he were to die then I would go to L.J. and help him in his cause …. so I did. As soon as I got word of his passing I started making my way to L.J. But I was very far away, so I knew it would take time. Fate is a funny thing, I got there the very day he was to be attacked by his Cousin and Uncle. I slipped into Ellen's ranks and disguised myself, then all I had to do is wait for my moment. A man by Ellen's side was told to go into the house to see what was happening. He came back and whispered something to her, it must have been bad news because she went off like a rocket, she went as far as to even kill the messenger. She then yelled to her men to set the house on fire. With that, she rode away in a fit of anger, thus giving me the opening I needed.

I got myself out of the group even easier than I got in. As soon as the fire was roaring, the rest of the men left. That's when I made my move inside. I searched the building and after what seemed like hours in the inferno, I found someone. He didn't strike me as L.J., the man before me was young, couldn't be any older than myself. As far as I knew Logan was into his 50's. However since he was the only person still alive, I dragged him out of the burning house and put him in the back of my Van. After he awoke, we both explained and introduced ourselves to each other, we discussed what happened to us that led us to that moment. With that finished we knew we must move quickly so we were on our way.

We knew we were too late to help Gastings, but since they were closest we had to go try. Once we got there we saw the destruction that had befallen this town. As we assessed the ruins, a man stopped us and told us to move on and not stay in this place of death. L.J. stepped in front to try and explain himself, after a brief conversation they walked back over to me, Logan introduced the man as John Simmons, an old friend of his. He told us that he and the men of this town wanted to join us and seek out the ones responsible for this destruction, thus preventing it from happening again to another town. With that we had the beginnings of an army. We made haste to Milton, the other town that was to be destroyed. Lucky for them, on this occasion we arrived in time to help.

We ambushed the would-be arsonists, dispatched them rather handily and continued on. We set up operation there in town, for the time being it was the safest and most secure place we knew of. So we came to the conclusion that it would be a very good command center. It also gave us the ability to protect these people from future attacks. Once we got settled, Logan went to look for Alexandra, one of the first people he had ever helped. When he got to her house he was given the news that she had died 5 months before after a serious bout of pneumonia. Logan did not take this news lightly. At this point, I was starting to get to know him very well. I knew it hurt him so bad to lose another person in his life. I tried to console him. He said he just didn't understand why any women he comes in contact with and cares about always seemed to die. I tried to tell him that death was a part of life and it had nothing to do with him, he was putting too much guilt on his shoulders. As I was calming him, I began to see the beauty of the man both inside and out. I saw the hurt he had gone through. I wanted to be with him to help him love again, as well as show him the love and emotion I was beginning to feel towards him. I gathered the courage to take a chance, I gently leaned in and kissed him. I am not really sure why, but I knew it was not as simple as me just getting lost in the moment. A new love was growing, one I just hoped he would accept.

I have to turn the story back over to L.J. Now, I have some matters to attend to.

As she said, I was totally devastated by the death of Alexandra , I just couldn't bare any more loss. As I was playing with the idea of closing everyone out of mt heart, Rebecca did an odd thing....She kissed me, when she did I felt....sparks. I haven't felt like that since Vanessa. Over the next 4 months our relationship evolved into a very strong love. It seemed right to me, she was a very similar person on many levels with Vanessa. It was as if the best qualities Vanessa had were mixed with best of my own and that created Rebecca. I will never know if Jack would approve but I would like to think that he would. It was right around the 4th month or so when we discovered that she was with child. We married that day in a very small ceremony. I was going to have a second chance at a family I lost in what seemed ages ago. Even with these new additions in my life, the mission would not change. Having a family is a hard thing for people like me, as great as it is to love and be given love back in return. It also places more responsibility on me. I knew I was going to keep them safe, I would not lose another family, I will not allow it again.

With Father in hiding and both sides building for the war we all know is coming, we are left with only one option. The gloves are off, if any members of the Family get in my way they will no longer be shown mercy, we tried to do it the easy way, but that time is now past. We have to find my Father and end this. The only way we can do this is ask the people closest to him, The Family, So be ready, soon we make our move, and while I do not know where this road may lead us. I know exactly where to start. And that would be the last person I knew for certain got an order from him. Ellen it is time you paid for your actions.

L J. Stevans

The Chronicles Of L.J. Stevans Part 16. A Healed Heart

Hello Again Friends,

I think it goes without saying that up to this point, my life has been.....unique to say the least. I lived almost an entire lifetime, and now I get to live the most formidable years once again. As crazy as it all seems, it has begun to sink in. I try to put it all into its proper perspective through my posts in the Chronicles or in talking to the people with me here in Milton. So many can live their lives in normalcy, never seeing the amazing things that are out there walking next to us but always just out of focus. I envy these people in a way, because they can just.....be. Keeping that in mind, I would never trade my life with any of them. We all have purpose, while everyone's purpose is important in many ways, it goes without saying that some have a greater impact on the world than others. I'm not trying to be a narcissist or anything, I know in the grand scheme of things a life is still a life. Aside from that there is also one *thing* that matters regardless the impact you may or may not have on the grand scheme of things. It is that *thing* that I think has been the best but still the most difficult for me..... love.

I am quite lucky, I have been madly in love twice. Recently a young man asked me a question about Vanessa and Rebecca that really got me thinking. He asked if the love I had and have for both women were equal. We have been here in Milton for months now and questions have become the norm around the town. Still it was a strange question to me, simply because I had never thought about it in those terms before. I knew I had to answer, just as I knew the question had more importance to this boy on the cusp of manhood. He was probably just starting to fall for a young lady out there and was looking for answers from someone objective and has for a fact been in love. By now everyone within the region has heard the story of what happened to Vanessa and what I did after, so I understand why it was me that he asked. Vanessa and Rebecca are quite different from one another in many ways save one. They both had a passion for life that was ever hungry, it is almost infectious.

I met both women in a time of duress, with Vanessa it was an instantaneous love, and that could be because we had no one else to turn to. I don't mean that in the way it may sound, we just knew that we met for a reason and we were all the other would ever have or need. Vanessa lived a life of servitude before I came along, everything was new to her, exciting and fresh. Everyday was an adventure full of new discoveries for her, and I just loved seeing her in the light of it all. Her joy brought me joy. Still, I knew my life was dangerous and yes, to this day I blame myself for hers as well as our unborn child's death. We decided to run, and live that way, we only stopped because we were not going to bring a baby in to that kind of life. We should have built a community and stayed safe within it, not on the outskirts of town like we did. But I never should have let the Family get to her, I should have taken the fight to them at that point, this is not a mistake I will make twice.

In the gap of time between the two relationships there was no one else, I just didn't want to get close again. I think it was the circumstances behind the meeting with Rebecca that gave the love a chance. After everything that happened at my house with my Uncle and Cousin and then receiving the gift of a second youth. I was very drained, physically and mentally. In this case it was Rebecca doing the saving, she got me out of that inferno, and got me to safety. She saved me and didn't even know that I was the one she was looking for. But that is who she is, she rights the wrongs, she has an adventurous nature, she is my equal in every way. Vanessa was more of the damsel in distress, not to say she was weak or not capable of taking care of herself, it's just she never had to. She went from her parents house to her "owners" house to being with me. Even at 5 months pregnant Rebecca wants to be in the fight we are about to enter with my Sister Ellen. She is an accomplished swords-women, but you would never know that by just looking at her. You would be surprised to find that she could knock you into next week. What she may lack in physical stature she more than make up for in will. She is just a bit shorter than I am, she is certainly not built like a fighter but not scrawny either. She is...well... she has...a voluptuous figure. Her body can accent any type of garb she may dress in. Her face is framed by two strands of hair that run down the sides just past her chin, with the hair in back going almost to the ground. So she normally keeps it in a tight bun of brown locks when fighting is near. I think it's her eyes that are the give away for her toughness, she has fiery eyes that could bring a giant to its knees. They are beautiful yet capable of staring a hole straight through you, take it from someone that has been on the wrong side of that gaze, it is not where you want to be.

In the fire I lost everything pertaining to Vanessa, it hurts to think about it but still she is with me. The love I have for Rebecca stands on its own, we are as one, soon to be as three. I tried to explain all of this to the young man with the question. Even though I think he was looking for a shorter answer, he still seemed to appreciate the fact I would open up in front of him. These people here are amazing, they not only welcomed us with open arms but also did so with the men that rode in with us, as well as the men that have joined us in the months we've been here. I know my family will be safe here as does Rebecca, even though she insists that she will be coming along in the battles that are ahead. She knows that nothing will happen to her here, I know I could not bare it if it did. It almost killed me the first time, I will not live through that again.

Even though I have suffered from loss in my other adventure into love, I was willing to allow it into my life a second time. I may not have thought I would find it again with the hectic life I live, but that's why Rebecca and I compliment each other the way we do. She is Jack's Daughter, the only other person I had real emotions for since my Mothers death. He was like a Father to me in many ways, as well as my best friend. Rebecca has all his best qualities along with his stubbornness. I think it was after I found out about Alexandra's passing, the way she was there for me. It was then she first kissed me, I knew it wasn't to get my mind off the troubles that plague me. It was because she *felt* my pain in that moment and connected with me, my heart is hers now, for however long she wishes to keep it. We are open and truthful with each other, I would be even if I was capable of lying. And yes, I have talked to her about Vanessa, aside from both loving me I think they would be fast friends. I think regaining my youth has something to do with the progress in healing my heart has made. It's almost like a second life, literally and metaphorically. It is a second chance, one I will not waste. I think that is the biggest difference between myself and my Family (save Ellen), they only love themselves and the power they can amass, I have loved deeper than any ocean. I know just how lucky I am. A man that has loved that deeply not once but twice, that is special indeed.

I left Ellen to the side of the Family when it comes to love and I did so for a reason. It was her order that took my Vanessa from me so I took her love from her as payment, which I now know is wrong. By doing so I created a monster incapable of ever loving again, she has waited a long time to strike against me. Soon she will have her opportunity, in the end she will just have to accept the consolation of being reunited with her Husband in death. While that may seem cold, it is just a truth, she will never let me live in happiness, we both know that. I gave her a chance to get out of this life, she didn't take it. Instead she held on to her hate and it is that hate that is going to put her into the ground once and for all.

L.J. Stevans

The Chronicles of L.J. Stevans: Part. 17. One Hand Washes the Other

-------------From Ellen-----------

To My Brother,

I feel that it is time to settle this Logan, don't you? I'm tired of the words and I'm bored with you, so I have a proposition for your consideration. I want you dead, plain and simple. However, I know that since our pain of a Grandfather has helped you with that gift of time, I can no longer do the deed myself. I want to settle this like it was in the ancient times. No massive war, no dramatic pointless loss of life on both sides. There is a much bigger storm brewing, you know it as well as I, so there is no point in throwing soldiers lives away now. This is about you and me, so here is what I propose. It will be you against a champion of my choosing. One on one, no tricks, you win and I go quietly to the authorities and turn myself in. If my champion wins, I get your life, meaning you come with me no questions asked. It is a fair deal, don't you think?

Ellen

------------20 Minutes Later-----------

To Ellen,

I wish I had a witty or sarcastic retort to insert here, sister. However, The chance to give you the death you deserve has almost left me speechless. So....Yes. I accept. The small field by Harper's Lake, three days from now, noon. You may bring 5 people with you as will I, but they are not there to fight, only to act as an insurance policy, nothing more. Do my terms satisfy you, sister?

L.J. Stevans

-----------10 Minutes Later------------

Agreed! Till then brother, enjoy your last days of life.

Ellen

---------------5 Days Later---------------------

To the World,

I wanted to write sooner but I have had to recover a bit from injuries I sustained during our latest battle. I have many questions I need to ask myself after this ordeal but none greater than this. Why would I do something so careless? I knew that her word was no good but I never expected this. I never thought that this would be a fair fight, or that it was just a ploy to hit Milton in our absence. That's why I got the town ready for an attack. I just never figured their tactics were this underhanded. I underestimated their treachery. This is a day that both sides can claim a victory. Although it is clear to me, that we were dealt the greater loss.

It started so simple, I picked those I wanted to be with me. I chose Rebecca, for no other reason than I just didn't have a option. Even with her days away from delivery, she insisted that she be there and that she was still the best marks-woman we had. I could not refute her claims. Along with her I took the two eldest sons of Alexandra's, Kyle and Henry. They were experienced and I trusted them. Last but not least there was John Simmons and the young man that asked me about love a while back, Brad, a boy of a mere 18 years. Brad has become like a shadow to me since that night by the fire, he has learned a great deal, along with the fact that he was very strong and more than capable in a fight. We arrived on the agreed upon location almost at the same time Ellen and her men did.

She and four men stayed on their hill, and a man could be seen walking down to the field. He was a tall thick legged man, maybe five inches taller than myself. He carried a giant hammer with an ax on the the other end, his arms pulsated as he moved it around. He was showing me that this weapon of his was not only heavy but that he was more than strong enough to wield it easily. I'm sure it also was a means of intimidation and if it was it was working. I looked over to Rebecca and her eyes were beginning to water. I hugged her and told her no matter what happens that she must put an arrow through Ellen's chest. She was not going to escape no matter what the outcome would be. I kissed her, it seemed to last minutes, I loved this woman so much that it pained me to pull away and head down to the fight.

We reached each other quickly, he said nothing to me. He just stood there nearly growling at me. I pulled my silver dagger from its sheath and reached for my short sword when I realized it was not there. In its place was a curved blade I knew well, it was Jacks sword, he called it Black Death. It was all dark black except for the edged side that was red as blood. I looked back to Rebecca and smiled at me. As I turned around I just managed to get out of the way of a sweeping hammer blow that would have ended me. I rolled back and regained my footing. I moved in and got him to swing again, he came downwards with the ax head this time, I side stepped it and countered. It went on like this for several minutes, I figured I could just wait and get him tired out but I was mistaken. He seemed to be getting stronger and more relaxed as we danced. I used a quick left to right step, he anticipated correctly and I was met with a blow from the hammer swatting me far to the left and to the ground. My arm was broken and I lost Black Death. It was then that I noticed this man was not crushing my skull in but looking up to the hill instead. As I followed his gaze to Ellen I realized something, this was a trap.

Ellen and her men started racing down the hill. All my group except Rebecca came down as well. I looked up just in time to roll away from the killing blow of Ellen's champions hammer, as it hit the ground I stabbed my dagger into his foot, he let out a mighty roar of pain. He brought his hammer back over his head in rage but as he did he left himself wide open. I found Black Death next to me I dropped my dagger as I went for the sword, I stabbed upwards slicing right through his belly. He fell back and then to the ground. I was getting back to my feet as the rest of our two groups collided in front of me. Ellen seemed to snarl at me as we rushed at each other. I only had one arm but I had to end this. As our swords rang against the other, I noticed she kept looking up to the hill where Rebecca was. A smile spread across her face, I knew then I had made a huge mistake. "What did you do?' I cried. "Nothing, brother. Father wanted to meet her, that's all." She laughed at me.

The next series of event, I did not see my self. I turned to run to Rebecca and Ellen put a bullet through my leg. I fell to the ground and rolled over just in time to see Ellen standing over me holding my Silver dagger. She brought the blade up high with the intent to drive it through my heart, as she was driving it down......I'll leave that part to Rebecca to explain.

-------------Rebecca sits down------------

I knew something was wrong when I saw Ellen and her men coming down the hill, I was so scared for Logan, I thought that brute had him for certain. I told the rest of our men to go down and help. I never thought that I would be in any danger, then again I never thought that this was nothing more than a set up. "So you must be Rebecca." I heard coming from behind me. I turned and saw an older man, a man that looked like L.J., just older and.... for a lack of a better term....devious. "Logan was a fool to bring you along and now he will suffer for it, and once again know the agony of loss." He started forward at me, sword drawn. A second voice stopped him in his tracks. "Stop" I heard someone yell out. As Logan Sr. turned to face the direction of the sound, I looked over and saw a white haired old man who again looked very much like L.J.. "Hello Father." Logan Sr. said flatly. "So is it time?" he calmly asked. The man I now knew to be the Historian nodded and came forth. "Help your husband girl!" He demanded of me. At that I turned and saw L.J. On the ground and hurt badly, I had to act fast.

-----------L.J. Takes a Seat and Continues-----------

Just as Ellen was bringing my own blade down to end my life, an arrow caught her directly in the chest, she fell to her knees. I started to rise up again, by this time my men had finished off the rest of hers and were coming to my aid. I order every one but Brad to go help Rebecca, I needed Brads help to get back to my feet and get me out of here. First I had one small piece of business to tend to. I looked to Ellen, she sat there on her knees clutching the arrow in disbelief. As I moved towards her to end this. She looked up to me with hate in her eyes, she spat at me and said "I will not give you the pleasure" as she slit her own throat with my silver dagger. She hunched over and died at my feet. I would not be recovering my dagger, it was now tainted with hate and anger filled emotions, let it follow her to Hell.

I heard the clashing of swords up by Rebecca, she was now starting to head down to me, the battle I heard was fierce but brief. We all met up together at the base of the hill and started back to the top. Rebecca told me of my Grandfathers assistance, I knew we had to hurry to him. When we got there, what we saw.....it will haunt us to our final moments of life. The Historian was impaled on a large broad sword. I approached him and was about to check for any signs of life, suddenly I was startled by him grabbing my hand. "Listen closely Logan, take this key, it is to my vault where the history of time is stored, the truth is there Logan. Do not let your Father take your essence. If he gets it, he will destroy everything. He is very powerful now, maybe too powerful. There may be another person that can help you. He is a MacStevans, and immortal, but he may be more myth at this point. Check the records in the vault. You are all that stands in his way. Your three remaining sisters will be coming for that key, keep it from them at all costs. You must find another to be The Historian now, I have left you a note, describing where to find the Immortal that is to be my successor, along with the location of the vault. You wanted answers about the world, you will find them there. The truth is your true gift ...use it...goodby....L...J.."

With those words he was gone.

The road just got harder but we will face it together. As we started back home, I realized just how much damage I took. I had to be carried back, and knew I needed medical help soon, Rebecca came close to me and kissed me, she held my hand and told me she loved me. I knew how much we lost that day, it could have been much worse. My arm will heal as will the rest of my wounds. I think it's the pain of loss that sticks with us the longest. I am thankful we did not lose more. I will always re...mem...ber......ummm....I am sorry friends I must go. Rebecca just grabbed my hand......It's time.......I'm going to be a Father!

L.J. Stevans

The Chronicles Of L.J. Stevans: Part. 18. Fatherhood And A Dangerous Understanding.

Hello Once Again World,

My life is now changed forever, it's funny that just under a year ago I thought fatherhood was nothing but a quickly fading dream. As I stood next to Rebecca holding her hand, I knew this was the most important moment of my life. Rebecca was in a great deal of pain of course, in fact she threw me out of the room.....twice. However she would quickly call me back to her side. Having a child in my life seemed foolish before I met Rebecca, after what happened to Vanessa can you really blame me? I think about how life could be if I am ever able to finish things with my Family. My mind gets lost in the idea all the time. There was no more time for such thoughts now, I stood there trying to be a anchor of strength for her. She was told to start pushing, so she did. The pain in her screams scared me and also created a new appreciate for not only the beautiful power women I have but also the fact that I am man. Moments later the doctor held up our new baby girl. I looked down at Rebecca and told her just how beautiful she was. The look of relief quickly turned to a look of confusion and pain, suddenly she started pushing again. The doctor seemed caught unaware by the new wave of screaming and pain. He went back to see what was happening and before I knew what to think of the events, he held up another baby....."It's a Boy!" He exclaimed.

Twins! We now had twins. My Family has a penchant for twins it seems. Rebecca now held both of our little miracles and looked down onto them with a tear in her eye and a new love in her heart. Until I saw the three of them, laying in that bed together, I never knew what unconditional love felt like. In a time of our lives that was filled with so much uncertainty, one thing became clear. My new mission in life was to ensure the safety of my new family.

Prior to the birth we had names picked out for either a boy or a girl, now we would get to use both. I picked up my son and looked into his still barely opened eyes and knew I was holding a James...... James Morgan Stevans. I knew his life would be hard because he is born with the same inability to lie that I have. Yet he will have something I never did, someone who understands him, and to show him the gift we both share. My wife looked at our daughter, then back at me and said. "Melissa Marie Stevans." I nodded with approval. With these changes to our lives it is important now, more than ever before, to look upon the problems and threats to our very existence.

The way I look at it there are four people left that stand in our way of freeing the region of mayhem and chaos. My father of course, and my three remaining sisters. My Father, we already know the basic plan and what the end game is for him. However, with the death of my Cousin and Uncle, I now do not know the *how* of this game. That is why it is so important to locate the Historians vault, gather as much information as we can and then find the new Historian to protect the truths of the world. This must be our first priority.

After that we should find the eldest MacStevans remaining, and see if he can lend his assistance. It all seems so simple, the order I mean. But as with everything in my life it is far more complex. We can't just go after the vault. The combined strength of my Sisters is far too great, and they could easily follow us and take possession of it, and that I cannot allow. I do not expect my Father will be coming out from whatever rock he is under for a while now. So, to me it seems simple. We stay put, allow Rebecca to regain her strength, and continue to build our Army that began to assemble here in Milton. Once they are strong enough to protect the town in our absence, we move out to track down my sisters. Besides, there is still plenty of things very close by that could benefit from our help. I still need to recover from the last beating I took, and a few....jobs... on the side never fails to bring a tad of excitement, training and not to mention coin into our lives. After all, now I have kids and schooling to think about.

Now, Bethany and Ellen were both, manipulating, sinister, and all around terrible people. Compared to my three remaining siblings however, they were saints. These are the three I was most worried about, they were not even in this region before now and I still had them in the front of my thoughts.

They are the ones in charge of the Family's dealing across The Great Eastern Ocean. At least they were, I received word a week ago that they have landed in our region and have already set up shop all around us. Aside from the fact that they are great leaders even have a good number of men at their disposal, they are....well ....they are Evil. capital. E. little. v. little. i. little. l. They are also well trained in all kinds of weaponry, but even if they were not they still form a more than formidable team. What makes them so dangerous is they simply have no regard for life. They murder, torture and punish all those in their path. I must take them seriously and expect anything from them. To do that I must reevaluate just who they are.

Amber, the eldest of the three. She is very tall, even taller than I am. She has short brown hair and almost golden eyes, she uses her looks to accomplish her will. Even at 45 she still is able to lure any man into her bed and right into her trappings. At least twice in her life she has intentionally tried and successfully gotten pregnant to hold a deal in place or ruin an uncorrupted mans image. This is how she operates, she uses treachery to take over any land, business or gang she chooses. She knows how to cast doubt in the mind of any person she meets, she can read and almost instantly understand any person or situation she comes in contact with. It is for these reasons she is known as the strategist of the Family.

Next up is Christine. Short and round, she is muscle of the group, it would be unwise to cast doubt on her abilities just from her appearance. She may be short and robust but she can pact a punch. She claims to have never taken a lover, though I would wager that it were a lover has never taken her. She can fight like a man and outlast any in a straight fight. Her face has never cast a smile, she always seems to be grimacing, but not in pain......at least not physical pain. They say she hears voices and is unstable, even the other two Stevans sisters are not brave enough to turn their backs on her. Her hair is stark white and that's not from age. The rumor/joke is that she is so evil, so depraved, so vile that even her hair has had the color drained from it in fear. Still she is not the one that worries me the most.

Abigail, she is the one to truly be aware of. She has the most power of the three because she not only possesses the worst qualities of the other two, but she also is the sole person in charge of the Family's army of followers. At 42 she is the youngest of the three and by far the most beautiful. Deep blue eyes and curly reddish-blonde hair the color of not quite ripe strawberries, frame her oval picture perfect face. She is of average height and her body is one of perfect proportion. She is a master of sword play, and the one in charge of every interrogation the family conducts. Her biggest skill however, may be her ability to find the right leverage points of a persons mind. Once found she then attacks without mercy. Even at her somewhat young age she has five teenage children, three boys, two girls and all born within a five year span. If it seems like she planned it that way, it is because she did. Each child born from a different father, she was said to have picked out the most physically and mentally fit male she could for mating. Directly after each birth the Father would simply disappear. Many call her the Mantis for these reasons. All five children are always at her side. They control the training of their men as well as provide security for their Mother and Aunts. Because of them she will be the hardest to gain access to.

They have no boundaries and it is said it's for that reason Father sent them over seas, he knew they would without a second thought kill the others to gain the power that constantly consumes their thoughts and drives their actions. While it is their strength that makes them all the more dangerous it also provides us with a weak point. Father does not trust them, not a shred. He knows they are looking for a way to live past this generation. Which can make them a threat to his Immortality. I know he will not aid them in their quest to find the vault, so it leaves me free to concentrate on them without worrying about his whereabouts for the time being. While the vault may hold the key to his Immortality he knows that inevitably, he is the lock. In truth, I'm not sure he is that wary of their plotting. He is still more powerful than all three combined, and he also just took the life of his own Father, an Immortal. My experience with Immortals tell me that he did so with knowledge that with the death of the Historian came with it more power in some form. And that is why he is never to be forgotten and always cautious of.

All of this talk is important and will help us in our quest for answers but for now I think it is best I go be with my family. Without them I have nothing, I know that now. They have given me something always missing from my actions in my first 50 plus years on this planet. Focus, unwavering responsibility and a sense of conviction in my belief that they are more important and precious than anything else in my life. I will do anything to keep them safe but at this moment I simply need to love them.

L.J. Stevans

The Chronicles Of L.J. Stevans: Part 19. Not Your Average Bandit

Hello Everyone,

Forgive me if I am a bit nervous, this is my first time addressing the Chronicles. My name is Bradley, but everyone calls me Brad. At the moment L.J. has business in the town, but since I was with him for the ride this morning, he wanted me to tell you all what happened today. To tell the truth it was pretty crazy to witness. It all started this morning, even before the sun had completely risen. A few of the townsfolk came to L.J. and told him of a lone bandit on the roads collecting "tolls" from passerby's. Since his last battle with Ellen's monster of a champion and the twins births he hasn't had any "action" as he refers to it. He was feeling almost a hundred percent so he said, and wanted to go out on a stroll for exercise and take a look at the would be "toll collector". Rebecca was still not ready to go out being only three weeks removed from the end of her pregnancy, and John was out fishing so I was hoping he would take me along. I know there is something that I do not quite yet understand about what happened today, but I will say this, Wesley Robbins is either the best or the worst highwayman I have ever seen.

The morning began simple enough. After breakfast, Logan came into my room and asked me if I wanted to check into this potential bandit situation. I jumped at the opportunity to do so. He has been asking me to go on most of his treks outside the town for a while now. So I have gotten better at controlling my outward enthusiasm a bit, but still, on the the inside I was still on cloud nine. I grew up listening to stories about him and now we are working together, it's still sinking in. He has really taken me under his wing. I don't have any family, they all passed on when I was ten. I made due, I guess. I worked at a tavern sweeping the floors, doing odd jobs around the bar and in return I got room and board until I was old enough to find real work and strike out on my own. So for L.J. and Rebecca to take me in and treat me as they do....well....it truly means a lot to me, I will do my best to never let them down.

After we got ready we moved out on horse back to the area we heard this bandit was located. Now I have known bandits and such men in the past, but I have never met one like this.

We came down the road and he just stood there, almost impatiently, like we were wasting his precious time. He didn't say a word. As we got closer, he just held up his hand in a halting manner. L.J. Signaled to me to remain mounted as he jumped of the horse to stand before this cocky man. L.J. walked over to him and simply asked him who he was. "I am L.J Stevans, your toll collector this morning. Just offer a worthy tribute for my single handed deed of making sure the bullies over at A. M. D. S. stays out of the area and you may be on your way." he brashly stated. Hearing his words I almost fell of my horse. L.J. just laughed a bit himself at this as he replied. "And just why would we do such a thing Mr. Stevans?" Without missing a beat this odd man began again. "Because I am L.J. Stevans good sir.

Have you not heard of me?" The man was not even sweating, it's as if he really thought he was L.J. "Of course I've heard of you, who hasn't? Sorry to have questioned you. Thank you ever so much for dealing with that foul company for us. What would you like sir?" L.J. baited the imposter. "Think nothing of it...." He started to say before being cut off by L.J.'s raised hand. "There is a small problem. How do we know you are who you say you are?" It's as if he anticipated the question and he responded to L.J. by pointing to his belt where L.J.'s famous silver dagger now resided. "You know of this dagger do you not." He retorted. L.J. again seemed amused by this, as he now started to put it all together. This man was a scavenger, he found the dagger, recognized it and realized he could make some good coin from its history. Now L.J. Was ready to put an end to this charade.

"Of course I know that dagger, I left it with my sister Ellen's body a while back. Now who are you really?" L.J. lightly prodded. The confidence now drained from his green eyes. Still he stood tall and composed, he almost matched L.J.'s height inch for inch. "Ah, I see. The rumors of your condition are not as accurate as I would have guessed." he started once again. "Yes, we didn't want people to know exactly what shape I was in." L.J. said as he again cut the imposter off. At this point I started to get nervous. The mans hand was moving slowly to his weapons but that's when I noticed so were L.J.'s. "Well, my name is Wesley Robbins, and I am a....service provider. I acquire difficult to come by items, as well as secrets. I am also a middle man for goods and services between small towns and groups." he said. He then popped his short curved blade as well as L.J.'s dagger up to his hands with a flourish. "I am also a master of the sword." L.J. seemed amused and brought Black Death and a new accompanying dagger to his hands. "OK, lets find out, I need the exercise anyway." L.J. responded as they went into their dance.

I had never been this close to L.J. while battling. His speed and form are much better than the stories suggest. However, this Wesley matched him move for move. The accurate swipes and counters rang out in the distance for several minutes until L.J. felt satisfied he got what he needed from the sparring session. He stepped back and sheathed his blades. I don't know if he thought his opponent would do the same, but he did not. He lunged at L.J. seeing the unarmed opponent as easy prey and was met with a kick to the side of his head that brought him down and sent his weapons out from his grasp. With that it was over. L.J. walked over to him, extended his hand and said. "I think we should have a talk."

I now dismounted my horse and followed the two men behind a tree where Wesley's cart was hidden. "So I don't need to ask you why you were pretending to be me. In the past, when times were tough I myself "collected tolls". So I understand your situation. However I cannot have you extorting money from the people in the area either. You haven't hurt anyone, so jail seems excessive. In light of that I have an offer to make you. I need some kind of a merchant and a link between the local towns and such, gathering supplies and information as well as a trained scout. Seeing that I also have not met a better swordsman in quite some time. I think you would make a fantastic sparring partner for myself and the boy here. Also there is one more thing. This may sound odd but just trust me, I want you to meet someone. I think it's important that you do." L.J. offered.

The proposal seemed to catch Wesley unaware. After a moment he responded. "So let me get this straight. I impersonate you, try to rob and then attack you. Your response to all this is to offer me a position in your camp?" L.J. just smirked. "Yes, that's what I'm offering you, maybe I'm slipping, or maybe I just know a valuable ally when I see one." he responded as he extended his hand. "I humbly accept, I take it you may want this back.", Wesley said without hesitation as he offered the silver blade back to its rightful owner.. L.J. looked at the blade a moment, seemingly getting closure with his decision to remain parted from the knife he had known throughout his life. "No you keep it. It seems to serve you better anyway. But since we are on the subject, you wouldn't by any chance have any other daggers, one with a little bit more of a ....WOW factor?" Wesley gave a nod. "Aah, a man who understands the need for showmanship, in fact I do. I have this little beauty here, its name is White Lightning. Please take it with my regards." he stated as he held out a rather long dagger with a menacing looking serrated edge side that complimented the bladed side. It looked like one side had the standard blade but the other was made into these sharpened teeth. L.J.'s eyes lit up as he happily took it, handled it a moment, feeling the weight before putting it in it's new home on his belt.

The three of us rode together back to town. Upon arrival the two new friends went off to talk. After a brief conversation L.J. walked him to his home where Rebecca was . He whispered something into Wesley's ear that made him stop in place and left him speechless. As L.J. showed him in I could only wonder what he said to him. After some time they emerged from the house, a look of shock and happiness now on Wesley's face. After a bit more talk L.J. then showed him where he could stay.....with me. I didn't mind. I had the room and frankly would enjoy some company. Logan told me that he wanted me to bond with him, watch him and learn the things he had to teach. He and I both agreed that he could indeed become a very valuable asset. Even though I can tell that there is obviously something more behind bringing him here.

Ah, L.J. is back, he wants to add something. I'll leave it to him then.

Bradley

Hello Friends,

It's funny, Wesley reminds me so much of myself, I think he will make a great teacher for Brad. He sees the greater good as do I. He has no love for the actions of my family. And you can never have too many strong connections in this day and age. The funny part to me is life's sense of humor, the chance encounters that we all have, that sometimes lead to something much bigger.

So Yes, there is one main reason above all others as to why I brought him in. In fact there is more to this man than as just another ally. I wanted to get him here without being asked too many questions. That's one of the burdens of not being able to lie, it's hard to surprise someone. So I just gave him reason after reason in hopes that he would not ask too many questions.

See I knew this man before today's encounter. I guess he didn't recognize me now that I am younger looking again. We met about five years ago, he was a teenager then, on the cusp of manhood and we were not introduced by name. It was a trip to a larger town back west that Jack and I were on. We were staying at a house of a women Jack had ......known. It was there where I met Wesley. The reason why he stood out to me was, that when we entered the house he greeted Jack as....... Father. Small world is it not?

The time for reflection and acceptance of the events that have transpired recently is now. Our Army grows larger by the day, with any luck not one of them will ever see battle. It is time to take back our own destinies, no matter the cost. Soon it will be time to find the vault and with it all the answers and new questions that will undoubtedly come with it. I for one will use this time to bond with my new children as well as our new friends. However, I will also train with the help of Wesley to become better in combat. I cannot take many more beatings like the one I suffered at the hands of Ellen's champion. I have relied on my instincts and reflexes alone far too often, I am sure they will fail me one day if I am not careful. These are all worries for another day, now.......now is the time, possibly our last opportunity to just be. And it is one that I will not let slip through my fingers. Adventure awaits us, as well the the inherent dangers that accompany it. For now however, I am just looking for a drink and my bed with the awaiting arms of Rebecca that accompanies *it*..... I may have accepted the role of a hero but I still am no saint.

L.J. Stevans

yes

i want morebooks!

Buy your books fast and straightforward online - at one of world's fastest growing online book stores! Free-of-charge shipping and environmentally sound due to Print-on-Demand technologies.

Buy your books online at

www.get-morebooks.com

Kaufen Sie Ihre Bücher schnell und unkompliziert online – auf einer der am schnellsten wachsenden Buchhandelsplattformen weltweit! Versandkostenfrei und dank Print-On-Demand umwelt- und ressourcenschonend produziert.

Bücher schneller online kaufen

www.morebooks.de